A Bit of a Hero

GERVASE PHINN

A Bit of a Hero

Andersen Press • London

First published in 2009 by
Andersen Press Limited
20 Vauxhall Bridge Road
London SW1V 2SA
www.andersenpress.co.uk
www.gervase-phinn.com

Reprinted 2009

British Library Cataloguing in Publication Data available.

ISBN 978 184 270 909 2

Mixed Sources
Product group from well-managed
forests and other controlled sources
www.fsc.org Cert no. TT-COC-0002227
© 1996 Forest Stewardship Council

Typeset by FiSH Books, Enfield, Middx.
Printed and bound in Great Britain by CPI Bookmarque, Croydon CR0 4TD

For my father, who for me was always a bit of a hero.

One

'Are you Count Dracula?' I asked innocently.

Dad had insisted that we visit the ruined abbey and St. Mary's Church perched high up on the cliff top. There was a magnificent view over the harbour from the church and a three-decker pulpit. I was not impressed with pews and pulpits nor keen to climb right up to the top of the cliff until Dad mentioned Count Dracula.

One hundred and ninety-nine steps later, we arrived at the church with the famous box pews and tall pulpit. I was in search of the vampire.

The vampire's dusty remains were brought to England in a ship with snow-white sails, he said, but it had been wrecked on the rocks just off the coast here. The black shiny coffin floated ashore and was hidden in the ruined Abbey by his evil servant. Late at night, the Count with blood-red lips and jet-black hair wandered around the churchyard, his sharp teeth shining in the moonlight.

When the vicar, a tall, thin, white-faced man in a flowing black cape appeared at the door of the church, it seemed obvious who he was. My red-faced parents hurried me down the steps until we were out of sight and then we laughed until we cried.

*

We had been in Whitby on holiday, staying at a cottage with creaky stairs, scratching mice behind the skirting boards, and a musty smell in the bedrooms. All I had left of my dad now was a photo which I kept by my bed.

I'd been awake for an hour but couldn't be bothered to get out of bed. I just couldn't take my eyes off my dad's face: I just stared at the photograph on the bedside table and wished he were still alive. He'd know what to do about the problem at school. He always knew what to do. He could always sort things out.

He smiled at me from the photograph with that great broad grin of his stretching from ear to ear. Mum used to say when he smiled like that he looked like a little boy who had just scored the winning goal. It was a sunshine smile.

I thought of Dad most at night before going to sleep. I went over and over in my mind all the things we used to do together. I remembered him shouting on the terrace at the football matches, waving his arms about as if he wasn't right in the head. Or diving underwater at the swimming baths and pretending to be a shark, grabbing my legs and snapping his teeth. Both of us sledging down Winnery Hill and rolling in the snow at the bottom. He taught me how to ride my bike, to hold a cricket bat, to bait a hook when we went fishing and to play chess. I could remember so many things we did together as clear as day. Now all I had of my dad were memories.

There was a tap on the door. 'Are you awake?' Mum poked her head around the door. 'It's nearly ten o'clock, young man.

You should be up and about on this bright Saturday morning.'

'I was just about to get up,' I said and lay back and closed my eyes.

'You look as if you are,' she said with a smile. 'And what are you up to today?'

'Nothing much,' I replied.

'Not going out with your friends?'

'No. My bike needs fixing.'

'Well, we could go into town this afternoon if you want and look for some new football boots. The ones you've got must be getting too small for you now.'

'Yes, OK.'

'And we could have some lunch at that café you like and maybe go on to see a film.'

'If you want.'

Mum stroked my shoulder. 'What's wrong, love?'

'I miss my dad,' I said simply. 'I really miss him.'

Mum sighed. 'I know, Tom. I miss him too.'

'It's like having this pain,' I said, 'that won't go away. I can't stop thinking about him. He's been dead for nearly a year now and everybody says it gets better but it doesn't get better. It gets worse.'

'Your dad wouldn't have wanted you to take on so, to go on grieving, now would he? He always tried to look on the bright side. "What's with the long face?" he used to say when you looked miserable or in a bad mood. He'd tell you to get on with your life, look to the future and remember the good times.'

I knew that Mum was putting on a brave face for my sake. I knew she was as grief-stricken and as in pain as I was. I'd heard her night after night sobbing away in the bedroom next door. I'd seen her suddenly go out of the kitchen halfway through a meal when something reminded her of Dad and rush up stairs and come down later with red eyes. I'd seen her look into space as if in another world and I knew she was thinking about Dad.

'And we did have some good times, didn't we?' she said, picking up the photograph and trying to smile. 'Do you remember where this was taken?'

'Whitby.'

'It was the best holiday we ever had, wasn't it? Staying in that spooky stone cottage with the rattling windows and great log fire. Do you remember when that mouse poked its head out of the skirting board? I screamed blue murder. Your dad wouldn't let me forget it weeks afterwards.' Mum shook her head. 'And it was in Whitby when you nearly choked on that marble. Do you remember?'

'Yes, I do.'

'You said you were pretending it was a sweet and it got lodged in your throat and you started to choke and your dad had to grab you round the chest and try to get you to cough it up.'

'And I swallowed it,' I said.

'And we had to take you to the hospital. I was really angry with you but your dad just found it funny. He couldn't stop laughing. You thought it would never come out and that

4

they'd have to cut you open but he told you not to worry. "People swallow things all the time," he said. Can you remember what your dad told you?'

'"What went in one way, should come out the other,"' I said. I smiled. I could hear him saying it.

'And we got that pink medicine in the brown bottle from the chemist,' continued Mum. 'It was such a job to get you to swallow it.'

'It was horrible,' I said, screwing up my face. 'All thick and slimy and it tasted of soap.'

'And the next morning you were sitting on the toilet—'

'You don't need to remind me,' I said.

Mum carried on regardless. '…and your dad and me were outside the bathroom door asking if anything had appeared and then we heard this clunk and you shouted out, "I've got my marble back," and your dad told you to leave it where it was. How he laughed.' She placed the photograph back on the bedside table. 'Well, come on, sleepy head,' she said, 'it's time you were up and about. You shouldn't be in bed on Saturday morning. And if you've nothing better to do you can help me tidy up the place a bit. Your Auntie Rita is coming round later.'

'Oh no!' I said, sitting up as if poked by a cattle prod. 'Why does she have to come around? I hate her.'

'That's not nice, Tom,' said Mum. 'You must never say that you hate someone. I know she can be a bit of a pain at times but apart from you, she's the only family I've got. Anyway she's been a lot better lately, after the row we had. Try and be nice to her for my sake.'

'You know what she was like after Dad died,' I said, 'coming round all the time, moaning and complaining and interfering and all those things she said about Dad. She was horrible.'

'Well,' sighed Mum, 'that's water under the bridge now. Just try and be a bit nicer to her. She's had her fair share of problems.'

'Huh,' I huffed. 'She's the problem.'

It's true what I told Mum. I do hate Auntie Rita. She's Mum's elder sister. Dad used to say that there are some people in the world who look for the best in others and then there are those who look for the worst. Auntie Rita comes into the second category. Everybody is wrong except her. Dad used to say that some people go through the world looking on the bright side, smiling and making the best of their lives and then there are others who moan and whinge and complain and blame everyone else for their misfortunes. Auntie Rita comes in the second category here as well. Dad used to say that it was incredible that she was my mum's sister because they were so different.

'Come along,' said Mum now, 'let's have you up. You can't stay in bed all day.'

When Mum had gone, I flopped back in the bed and stared up at the cracks on the ceiling. 'Auntie Rita,' I mouthed. 'That's all I need.'

I hadn't told Mum the whole truth about why I was feeling so upset and miserable. It would only worry her. I really was missing my dad, that was true, but there was the other thing that kept preying on my mind. I was frightened.

Martin Roadhouse, a new boy, had arrived at school two weeks before and it soon became clear to everybody that he was bad news. That very first morning, as he sat there leaning back on his chair grinning, I knew there was going to be trouble. You would think that someone starting a new school with all those new faces would be a bit shy and scared. I know I would have been. Martin Roadhouse wasn't.

When Miss Fairclough, our teacher, called the names on the register we all answered: 'Yes, miss. Good morning, miss.' Martin Roadhouse must have heard most of the class reply like this so he knew what to say, but when the teacher read out his name, he stood up, tapped his forehead and replied in a really loud and surly sort of voice, 'Aye, Aye, Cap'n!' Miss Fairclough put down her pen, smiled and told him really nicely how to reply. He puffed out his cheeks, blew out a mouthful of air noisily and said, 'Okey-dokey, teacher.' Miss Fairclough ignored him but I could see she was angry. She reminded the class that there would be a band and choir practices the following Wednesday and Thursday lunchtimes.

'Perhaps you'd like to learn an instrument and join us, Martin,' she said. When he told her that bands and choirs were for cissies, I knew there was going to be trouble.

Miss Fairclough had to tell him off four times the very first morning – for stabbing the desk with his pencil, not concentrating on his work, for chewing, and for coming in

7

late after morning break. He didn't seem to mind a bit, but looked her straight in the face with an insolent smile.

It was during the second week that the bullying began. Martin Roadhouse started by calling people names; then he crept up behind them on the corridor, kicked their heels or poked them in the back. He'd grab bags and tip out the contents, looking for sweets. Nobody did anything because he was so big. He looked more like fourteen than eleven with his round pudding face, mop of dusty looking hair, fingers as fat as sausages and his huge lumbering body. I kept well out of his way all week but I knew I couldn't avoid him forever and that my turn would come. Last Friday it did just that.

Two

Although nearly twelve months had passed since that awful day when they came and told Mum and me that Dad had died in the fire. I remember it as if it were yesterday. I came home from school in a really good mood because I had scored the winning goal in a football match with St Joseph's, to find two police cars parked outside the house. Mum was in the kitchen with a hand over her mouth and her face was all red and puffy. A woman in uniform was trying to comfort her and stroking Mum's back. I remember Mum pulling me to her and sobbing into my chest, great heaving sobs, and trying to tell me, between gasping for air, what had happened. I remember the policeman telling me to be brave, that Dad was a hero and that Mum needed me now more than ever. It was as if my world had just fallen apart.

Then there was the funeral. The church was packed and there were lots of people I had never seen before. Dad was a firefighter and everyone from the station was there, dressed in smart black uniforms and looking really sad and some a bit embarrassed about what to say to me and Mum. Dad's closest friends were crying. Six stony-faced officers carried in the coffin. Auntie Rita, of course, sat at the front of the church next to Mum and me, taking centre stage, dressed all in black and looking like the wicked witch at a pantomime. After the funeral we went back to a cold and empty house.

Of course, it didn't sink in that Dad had gone, that I would never see him again. I kept expecting to hear his voice shouting up the stairs for me to get out of bed or telling me I was too long in the bathroom or hear him whistling when he worked in the garage. I expected to come down for breakfast in the morning to find him sitting at the table with his big mug of tea and great smile. Life without Dad was like some horrible dream, some nightmare from which I would one day wake up. But I will never wake up from it. Never.

A couple of weeks after the funeral Mum and me went down to the Fire Station and Mum was presented with a medal by the Chief Fire Officer. Dad had had lots of commendations in his time, but this medal was really special. The Queen's Medal it was called. It was for bravery and only awarded on very special occasions. Mum said I could have it. She said Dad would have wanted me to have it. I put in on my bedside table below the picture of my dad standing outside the fire station in his uniform, beaming at the camera as if there were no tomorrow and next to the photograph taken at Whitby. Of course, for Dad, there wasn't a tomorrow. Sometimes I would wake up in the night and see his smiling face and his medal gleaming in the moonlight. Then I would cry myself back to sleep.

Then, after Dad's funeral, Auntie Rita arrived and took charge. I arrived home from school one day to find her at the kitchen sink, puffing away on a cigarette. Dad never allowed anyone to smoke in the house and she knew it. He used to say that it was a dirty, expensive habit and a health hazard as well.

More fires were caused by people leaving smouldering cigarettes about the place than anything else. Dad, as a firefighter, knew what he was talking about.

'What are you doing here?' I asked her.

'Nice welcome, I must say,' she said, blowing out a cloud of cigarette smoke. She put on a really sarcastic voice. 'Oh, hello, Auntie Rita, how nice to see you. How are you, Auntie Rita? How have you been keeping, Auntie Rita?'

'Well, what are you doing here?' I repeated.

'I'm here to help your mum,' she said, tapping the ash from her cigarette in the sink. 'What do you think I'm here for?'

'She doesn't need any help,' I told her.

'Oh, yes, it looks like it,' she said, glancing around the kitchen and taking another puff of the cigarette. 'This place needs a good clean.' She ran a finger along the surface next to the cooker. 'Grease and grime everywhere. Dust on everything. Just look at—'

'We like it like this,' I interrupted.

'Well, I don't,' she said.

'Yes, well, it's not your house, is it, so we can please ourselves what we do.'

'You want to watch your tongue, young man,' she said, stabbing the air with her finger. 'Too cheeky by half, you are. You've had it too easy.' She stubbed out the cigarette in the sink. 'You should show more respect. Got away with murder you have. Being waited on hand and foot. Well, you'll have to start pulling your weight from now on. I'm here to help your mum and I'm not your skivvy, so don't think I'm tidying up after you.'

'I didn't ask you to tidy up after me,' I replied, 'so why don't you go home?'

'And don't you get clever with me. You're not too old to get a good hiding.'

'Huh!' I snorted. 'You want to try it.'

'Now look—' began Auntie Rita.

'And we don't allow smoking in this house,' I told her.

'Says who?'

'Dad.'

She shrugged. 'Yes, well, your dad's not here any more, is he?'

At this point Mum wandered in. She looked deathly pale, hair stuck up like a brush and she had dark rings beneath here eyes. 'What's all the noise?' she asked wearily.

'Now look what you've gone and done!' snapped Auntie Rita. 'Waking your mother up. Just put her head down for a little nap and you go shouting and creating trouble.' She put an arm around Mum's shoulder and helped her to a chair as if she were an invalid. Mum looked like an old woman.

'Do we have to have her here?' I asked Mum.

'Your Auntie Rita's here to help out, love,' Mum replied, running her hand through her hair. 'Just until I can get back on my feet.'

'I don't want her here!' I exclaimed.

'What you want and what you'll get are two different things,' said Auntie Rita. 'Now stop upsetting your mum. I don't know what's got into him. Answering me back—'

'He's lost his father, Rita,' said Mum quietly.

That shut her up.

'I'm going up to my room,' I told them.

'What about your tea?' asked Mum.

'I don't want any, I'm not hungry,' I told her.

'Suit yourself,' Auntie Rita shouted after me as I walked out of the kitchen.

Later that night, when Auntie Rita had finally gone, Mum brought some sandwiches and a glass of milk up to my room. The bread was stale and the milk tasted sour. Mum didn't notice, of course. She sat beside me on the bed.

'I know it's hard for you, Tom,' she said, 'but try and be nice to your Auntie Rita, for me. I know she can be difficult but she's only trying to be helpful.'

'But why do we have to have her here?' I asked. 'We're all right as we are.'

'Don't start, please,' said Mum. 'I've already told you she's helping out just until I get back on my feet. I can't think straight at the moment. Everything's just got on top of me. I'll be fine soon.' She didn't sound that convincing.

'I'm sorry, Mum, but I'm feeling awful as well. I can't think straight either. I can't keep my mind on things. I really miss him. I really miss my dad.' Then I burst into tears.

Mum pulled me to her and held me really tight. 'I know love,' she said, 'I know.'

Those few weeks after Dad died were the worst weeks of my life.

*

I never used to like school much. I am at Holgate Primary School, which is only ten minutes walk around the corner from our house. I never found the work particularly hard and I liked seeing my friends and playing football in the playground and in the team against other schools on Saturday mornings, but I can't say I looked forward to walking up the path every morning. I would have much preferred to be riding my bike up to the ruined castle at Winnery Hill or exploring the woods at Snape or watching the trains come screeching through the tunnel at Roper's Crossing or cheering Sheffield United on the terraces.

'School days are the happiest days of your life,' Dad used to say. 'Make the most of them.' I never used to think that.

Then Miss Fairclough arrived. She's great, Miss Fairclough. She makes learning about things really interesting and is friendly as well and good fun. Everyone in our class likes her. She's the best teacher in our school. She's only young, straight out of college, my dad had said. He said teachers weren't like that when he was a lad. 'I wouldn't have been able to keep my mind on my work,' he once told me, 'with Miss Fairclough looking at me all day with those big dreamy blue eyes.' Then he winked. 'And don't tell your mum I said that.' Miss Fairclough has long hair like Rapunzel in the fairy story but has it tied back when she's in school. Once Dad and I met her in town and her hair was like a curtain of gold.

When Dad was killed she called round to our house with some flowers and a card. Mum said later that it had been really thoughtful of her to take the time and the trouble.

14

'Miss,' I asked Miss Fairclough the week after Dad died, 'can I stay and help after school?' I hated going home to find Auntie Rita there and the less I saw of her the better.

'Of course you can, Tom,' she said. 'I have to finish off the display and could do with another pair of hands.'

I had just finished cutting out the last piece of coloured paper, when she asked me, 'And how are things at home, Tom?'

'OK, miss,' I lied.

'How's your mum coping?'

'OK,' I said.

'And how are you coping?'

'I'm all right, miss,' I replied.

'Are you?'

'Yes, miss.'

'Are you sure?'

'I'm fine.' I wanted to tell her the truth, how awful and empty I felt, but the words just wouldn't come out.

'Because if ever you want to talk about anything, I'm a very good listener.'

'I'm all right, miss, really,' I told her, wishing she wouldn't go on about it.

'It must be dreadful losing a father,' she said sadly. 'I know how you must feel.'

'Did your father die when you were a girl, miss?' I asked.

'Well, no,' she said. I could tell she was a bit embarrassed by the question. She went red and looked suddenly hot and flustered. Then she said, 'My father's still alive. What I meant was that I can sympathise. I know what you must be going through.'

As I said, she is nice is Miss Fairclough and means well but there was no way that she knew what I was going through. Only those who have lost a parent know what it feels like. Only those who have had their world turned upside down, who see their mum change overnight, who have to cope with the fact that they will never ever see their dad again, grow up without him being there, really know what it feels like.

'We've missed you at the last band practice,' she said, changing the subject and trying to sound cheerful. One of the first things Miss Fairclough did after she arrived at the school was to start up a brass band and a choir. Music was her subject at college. I was learning to play the trumpet. It was only a small group but it was fun. Dad played the tenor horn in the Listerdale Mill Firefighters' Brass Band and he was really pleased when I took up the trumpet. He would play along with me sometimes when I practised. He hoped that one day I would join him in *his* band. There was no chance of that now. I stopped playing the day he died.

'Pardon, miss?' I asked.

'We've missed you at yesterday's band practice,' she repeated. 'I'm afraid your friend Sinclair tends to play more wrong notes than right ones. He could do with a bit of help.'

'I don't feel like it at the moment, miss,' I told her.

'Well, I hope you've not decided to drop out. You are a good little player.' I didn't answer. 'Think about it,' she said. 'Now, come along, Tom, it's time you were getting on home. Your mum will be wondering where you've got to. And remember, if you do want to talk about anything I'm always here.'

Thinking back to those first few weeks after Dad's death one of the things I remember most was how nice Miss Fairclough had been compared with Auntie Rita. I could sometimes see my teacher looking at me in class and I knew that she was worried about me and she never missed an opportunity of having a word and asking me how I was. Never once had Auntie Rita asked me how I felt or how I was coping. It was all 'Do this' and 'Do that'. That's one of the reasons I dislike her so much. After the conversation with my teacher that afternoon, I arrived home and Auntie Rita was still there. She was watching television in the front room, a cigarette smouldering on a saucer in front of her and a mug of half-drunk coffee on the floor. The house looked exactly as it had done that morning. Some cleaner, I thought.

'And where have you been?' she asked, not even bothering to look away from the television screen.

'At school,' I told her. 'Where do you think I've been?'

'Not till this time, you haven't.'

'I've been helping my teacher, if you must know.'

'Oh, well, let's hope it's catching,' she said, reaching for the cigarette. 'Your room could do with a tidy.'

'I don't want you going in my room,' I snapped.

'Really?' She sucked at the cigarette.

'I like it as it is.'

'Well, don't think I'm cleaning up after you. If you want to live in a pigsty then it's up to you.'

17

'Where's Mum?' I asked.

'She's having a sleep, so don't disturb her.'

I went up to my room and on the way I popped my head around Mum's bedroom door. She was curled up in the middle of the bed, sleeping.

At tea time I gobbled down the food as fast as I could. I didn't want to spend any more time than I had to in the company of Auntie Rita. She sat opposite Mum at the kitchen table, ignoring me and rabbiting on to Mum, smoking like a chimney.

'So what do you think?' she asked Mum.

'I'm sorry, Rita, what did you say?'

'I said do you fancy going to the cinema one night this week? It'll take you out of yourself.' She nodded in my direction. 'He'll be all right on his own.'

'No, I couldn't face it at the moment,' said Mum. She stared down at the half-eaten meal.

'Well, you can't hide yourself away like a hermit for ever, Margaret. I mean you've not been out of the house since the funeral. I don't want to sound hard, but life does go on, you know.'

Mum looked up and stared at Auntie Rita for a moment. 'I know life goes on, Rita,' she said, 'and that's what makes it so hard.'

'I mean, it's terrible what happened to your Jimmy, terrible. No one's denying that. It was awful. A real tragedy. Mind you, as I've said to you before, I can't for the life of me understand why it was him who had to go back into that burning house.

What were all the other firefighters doing?'

'Because that's what Jimmy was like, Rita,' said Mum. 'He was always at the front of the queue when it came to helping anybody.'

'That's as may be,' said Auntie Rita. 'Anyway, what's done is done. We can't undo the past, much as we would like to. You've got to get on with your life, think about yourself. You've got to try and pull yourself together. You can't let yourself go to seed. You've got to try and sort out your life, decide what you are going to do. I mean, when I was deserted I felt just like you, that my world had come to an end.'

Mum looked over at me. 'Have you finished, Tom?' she asked.

'Yes,' I replied.

'Then you can go up to your room. I'm sure you don't want to sit here listening to me and your Auntie Rita.'

I did want to sit there listening to Mum and Auntie Rita. It was just getting interesting. But I put my plate in the sink and left the kitchen.

'And you can come down later and wash these things up,' Auntie Rita shouted after me.

I stood behind the door to listen to their conversation.

'Look, Rita,' said Mum, when she thought I was out of hearing, 'I'm sure you mean well, but Paul walking out on you and Jimmy being killed are hardly the same thing.'

'I was just saying—' began Auntie Rita, but Mum cut her short.

'Paul and you were never happy together. You didn't get on over the last few years. You were always bickering, always at each other's throat.' Well, that wasn't true, I thought. I couldn't remember a lot about my Uncle Paul but I do remember that every time they came round it was Auntie Rita who did all the bickering. He just sat there and sighed. 'Jimmy and I had a very happy marriage,' Mum continued.

'It was by no means easy for me, Margaret,' said Auntie Rita sharply. I could imagine her bristling like an angry cat. 'Being left to cope by myself, bringing up Barry and getting precious little thanks for it. Up and walks out on me like his dad. And hardly a word from him. Couple of postcards during the year and a Christmas card, that's all and the rare visit if he happens to be in the area. That's as much as I get from Barry. It wasn't a bed of roses, I can tell you, when they up and walked out. And when I think of all the time I've spent—'

'I'm not saying it was easy for you, Rita,' interrupted Mum. 'I know it was hard on you but your situation and mine are entirely different.'

'Well, I know that. I didn't get any big payout like you for a start. I mean, it's not as if you have to work any more what with the compensation you got.'

'I think you had better go, Rita,' said Mum. 'I'm tired and I'm going to have a lie-down.'

'I'll be off then,' she said. 'And you want to get that son of yours to watch his manners and pull his weight.'

When I heard the chair scraping on the kitchen floor – the

20

signal that she was coming my way – I hightailed it up to my room.

After that Mum did seem to pull herself together. Auntie Rita didn't call round as often and that suited me. I still missed Dad terribly but without the Ugly Sister filling the house with stinking cigarette smoke and interfering in everything, I began to feel a lot happier. Then Martin Roadhouse came into my life.

Three

It's amazing how one person, just one single person, can change so many people's lives and cause so much trouble and in so short a time. At first we were all friendly towards him. Miss Fairclough told us to make the new boy feel at home and we tried to do that but he soon showed his true colours. He was a bully. He didn't single any one person out for bullying at first, he picked on everyone so that after a week nobody wanted to work with him in class or play with him in the school yard, nobody wanted to sit with him at lunch time and we only spoke to him if we had to. We all tried to keep well out of his way. But then he started to single people out.

Simon, one of my best friends, has a stutter and it wasn't long before Martin Roadhouse started mimicking him. 'Ssssimple Sssimon sssstutttters,' he said to him in the yard, pushing his fat face into Simon's and spitting out the words. 'Wwwat a ssshame.'

Then he picked on Charlotte Simcox, who has red hair and freckles. 'Here comes Spotty Simcox!' he shouted at her when she came into the classroom one morning before the teacher arrived.

He had left me alone until Friday, but when I saw him staring at me across the classroom with a sick smile on his face I knew that my time had come.

Miss Fairclough found it really difficult to deal with Martin

22

Roadhouse that particular day. He had been troublesome all week but on Friday he was worse, always out of his seat disturbing people, making clever comments, laughing really loudly, anything to avoid doing any work.

'Martin,' said Miss Fairclough, 'will you please sit down and get on with your work.'

'It's boring,' he replied. Then he yawned really widely.

'Is it really?' asked Miss Fairclough, trying to keep patient.

'Yeah, it's really boring. I don't feel like writing soppy poetry. Poetry's for cissies like Sinclair.'

'I'm not interested in your opinions, Martin,' said Miss Fairclough, 'and kindly keep your unkind comments to yourself. Now sit yourself down and get on with your poem.'

'It's boring,' he replied. 'I've told you.'

'Martin,' said Miss Fairclough, gripping the edge of her desk, 'if you do not sit down this minute and get on with your writing, you'll stand outside Mrs Reece's door.' Mrs Reece was the head teacher and having to stand in the corridor outside her room in full view of everybody was a dreaded punishment. It didn't seem to worry Martin Roadhouse though.

'I'd sooner stand outside her door than write soppy poetry,' he replied. 'It's all la-di-da and bloody daffodils.'

'Don't you dare use that kind of language in my classroom!' the teacher shouted. 'Go and see Mrs Reece immediately.' She pointed to the door and I could see her hand trembling. 'Go on.'

'What?' he asked, not moving.

'Go and stand outside Mrs Reece's door and tell her that you refuse to do the work I have set.'

'I don't feel like going, now,' he said.

It was like watching some really exciting television programme that you just could not turn off. All our eyes kept moving backwards and forwards from Miss Fairclough to Martin Roadhouse.

'Well, I am telling you to go,' said the teacher, now standing behind her desk and pointing to the door. 'And you will stay there until Mrs Reece tells you to return.'

'Big deal.'

There was a deathly silence in the room.

'What did you just say?' asked Miss Fairclough. She seemed to balloon with anger.

'I said, "Big deal."'

'Get out!' shouted Miss Fairclough. 'Now!'

He smirked, got to his feet and with slouching shoulders, ambled out of the classroom.

With Martin Roadhouse out of the way there was a great sigh of relief from everybody. We got on with our work extra quietly. Miss Fairclough looked upset and sat at her desk breathing heavily. She was really red in the face. We had never seen her lose her temper like that before or look so upset. I felt really sorry for her.

After morning break Mrs Reece brought Martin Roadhouse back to the classroom. Her mouth was all screwed up as if she were sucking a lemon.

'Return to your desk, Martin Roadhouse,' she ordered,

pointing a bony finger before her, 'and get on with your work.' He lumbered across the room and plonked himself down heavily on his chair. He didn't look at all bothered. 'Not a very good start in a new school, is it?' She didn't really expect an answer because she carried on talking. 'Only just arrived and you're in trouble. I sincerely hope this is not a taste of things to come. I do not want to see you outside my door again. Is that clear?'

He looked up at her with a silly smile on his fat face. 'Yes, miss,' he answered sweetly.

'And what have you got to say to Miss Fairclough?' asked the head teacher. 'Sorry, miss, for being rude,' he said, again in a sickly sweet tone of voice.

'And you will stay in over the lunch hour,' continued Mrs Reece, 'and catch up on the work you have missed. You will bring it to me at the end of the day. If it is not satisfactory you will stay in every break until it is. Is that understood?'

'Yes, miss,' he said.

Later that morning when Miss Fairclough was helping Shruti Patel with her writing, Martin Roadhouse passed a note to Sinclair. I was sitting next to Sinclair and could read the large scrawly writing clearly. It said: 'Rite a pome skwirt for me to copy out or U R DEAD!!!!'

So, Sinclair wrote him a poem which he copied out and took to Miss Reece at home time and Martin Roadhouse got himself out of trouble.

I was coming out of school with Sinclair that awful Friday afternoon, talking about how Sheffield United would get on

25

in the match the following day. We had just turned the corner of Ramsden Road when we heard a voice we dreaded.

'Oi!'

It was Martin Roadhouse.

'Carry on walking,' said Sinclair, speeding up. I could see he was frightened. 'Pretend we haven't heard him.'

'Oi!' came the voice again. 'I'm speaking to you two, little squirts.' We stopped and heard him lumbering up behind us. He prodded Sinclair in the back. 'Got any sweets?' he demanded.

'No,' said Sinclair. There was a tremble in his voice.

'Bet you have,' said Martin Roadhouse.

'I haven't,' said Sinclair, quickening his step.

'Let's have a look.'

The bully grabbed Sinclair's bag and tipped everything onto the ground. 'What's this?' He picked up some coins, which had spilled out. 'This should buy us some sweets.'

'That's my bus fare,' cried Sinclair.

'Oooo, that's my bus fare,' mimicked the bully. 'Well, you'll just have to walk home, won't you, squirt.'

'My mum'll get worried,' Sinclair told him. 'I always get home for half past four. She'll wonder where I am. It's a mile walk.'

'Oh dear, Mumsie will get worried,' said the bully in a silly wheedly sort of voice. 'Tough!'

'Please don't take my money,' pleaded Sinclair.

'Get lost!' said the bully. 'And I want some more next week, so come prepared.'

Then he turned his attention to me. 'And what you staring at, Speccy-four-eyes?'

'Nothing.'

'You're the kid whose dad was killed, aren't you?' His eyes were like slits on his fat pudding face.

'Yes.' I felt my heart banging away in my chest and I could feel my face getting hot.

'I heard about that. It was in all the papers. "Firefighter dies in tragic blaze".' His voice was mocking. 'Everybody said he was a hero.' I wanted to say that he was, but I didn't answer. I was scared. 'Well, do you know what I think? I think he was stupid, that's what I think. He must have been really dumb going into a blazing building.'

'What did you say?' I asked quietly.

'I said, I think he was stupid going into a house that was on fire.'

'You take that back!' I cried.

He threw his head back and laughed. 'And are you going to make me, Speccy-four-eyes?' He poked me really hard in the chest. 'I could spit on you and drown you.'

Sinclair was busy picking up all his books and pens and stuffing them in his bag. I could see that he just wanted to get away as fast as he could.

'My dad was a hero,' I said. My mouth was dry and my voice sounded all weak and croaky. 'He tried to save somebody's life.'

'Well, I say he wasn't!' trumpeted the bully. 'I say he was stupid and dumb. Dumb! Dumb! De Dumb!'

27

'Come on,' said Sinclair, pulling at my sleeve. 'Just leave it.'

'Yeah, go on, Speccy-four-eyes, before I knock your stupid glasses off your stupid face.'

I walked away, panting with anger and with tears in my eyes. I hated myself. I felt such a coward, walking away and hearing the bully's loud laughter behind me. I felt ashamed of myself.

'Ignore him,' said Sinclair, gripping my arm. 'Just forget about it. Bullies are sad, sad people. They like hurting you and if they see it upsets you they do it more and more. It's best not to take any notice.'

But I couldn't forget about it. That night in bed I couldn't get the words out of my mind. 'He was stupid going into a house that was on fire.' That's what Martin Roadhouse had said. Then Auntie Rita's voice got into my head, eating away like a maggot in a rotten apple: 'I can't for the life of me understand why it was him who had to go back into that burning house. What were all the other firefighters doing?'

I lay there staring at the cracks on the ceiling, saying again and again, 'My dad was a hero. My dad was a hero.'

He went into a blazing house to rescue a little girl. I remembered the newspaper article. It covered the front page. Someone had left a towel drying by the fire and it had caught alight. When the fire brigade arrived the house was full of flames and choking smoke. Dad and the other firefighters had gone in and pulled a woman and two children out but she had started screaming that her little girl was still inside. Dad had run back in. The roof had fallen on him. He was killed. I had been over and over it in my mind and now I was doing it again and asking myself why did it have to be my dad? Maybe Martin Roadhouse was right. My dad might have been stupid to go back in. Most people wouldn't. Why did he have to go back into the house? Why didn't he stay outside and tell himself he couldn't do anything? Why did he go and get himself killed? Auntie Rita's words echoed again in my head: 'I can't for the life of me understand why it was him who had to go back into that burning house. What were all the other firefighters doing?'

I wished so much that Dad were there to tell me what to do. But he wasn't.

Four

When I got downstairs that Saturday morning when Mum and me had talked about our holiday in Whitby, I found Auntie Rita in the kitchen, sitting at the table by herself with a cup of tea in front of her and a cigarette dangling from her lips. She sucked in and blew out a cloud of smoke.

'I see the Sleeping Beauty's woken up,' she said.

I ignored her and opened the fridge.

'If you're after milk, there is none,' Auntie Rita told me. 'Your mum's popped out to the corner shop to get some. I said to her that if it was up to me I'd get you out of bed to fetch it. I can't say that you do all that much around the house, not as far as I can see. She spoils you does your mum. I've always thought so.' I was tempted to say what Dad sometimes used to say: 'You know what thought did, it followed a manure cart and thought it was a wedding' but I ignored her and got myself a glass of water.

'Do you have to smoke?' I asked. 'It's a dirty habit and you stink the place out. Smoking can kill you.'

'Hark at doctor know-it-all,' she said, continuing to puff away at the cigarette.

I left her in the kitchen and headed back to my bedroom.

'Going back to bed, are we?' she shouted after me as I climbed the stairs.

When I was back in my room I realised I had left my

school books in the front room. The last thing I wanted was Auntie Rita looking though them so I went back downstairs. Auntie Rita wasn't expecting me, of course, and that's when I caught her red-handed. She wasn't in the kitchen but in the living room, poking through the papers in the small bureau. Mum and Dad kept all their important documents in the bureau – boring stuff like the TV licence and post office books, bills and receipts – and I was not allowed to go in there. Now I found Auntie Rita rootling though the papers. It was private. And there she was going through everything.

I stood at the door watching her for a moment. She didn't see me, so busy was she shuffling through the contents in the bureau.

'What are you doing?' I asked eventually.

It was as if someone has poured a bucket of ice-cold water all over her. She jumped about a foot in the air, before putting her hands to her throat and gasping like a fish out of water.

'Will you not creep up on people like that!' she spluttered. 'You gave me the shock of my life.' She stuffed the papers back into the bureau and banged the drawer shut. She had a really guilty look on her face.

'What are you doing?' I asked again.

'What?'

'I said, what are you doing?'

'I was looking for something,' she said.

'What?'

'What do you mean, what?'

'What were you looking for?'

'An envelope, if you must know.'

'What for?'

'What's this, the third degree? I was looking for an envelope, all right?'

'No, it's not all right. You were looking through Mum's private things. I'm not stupid. I saw you poking through all her papers and reading them. You were snooping. I saw you.'

'Don't be so daft,' said Auntie Rita, colouring up. 'What would I want to do that for?'

'Because you're nosy and interfering, that's why.'

Her face went really red now and her mouth became small and tight. 'You want to be careful what you say, accusing people. I've had just about enough of you. You're a nasty, selfish, ungrateful little boy and you want a damn good hiding. Spoilt, that's what you are. You wander about the house without a by-your-leave, expecting your mother to be at your beck and call. You treat this house as if it was an hotel. If it wasn't for your mother being so upset, I'd have a few well-chosen words to say to her about you.'

'Yes, and I'm going to have a few well-chosen words to say to her about *you*, looking though all her private papers.' I went over to the settee and sat down and folded my arms tightly over my chest. 'And I'm staying in here till Mum comes back.'

'You can suit yourself,' said Auntie Rita, returning to the kitchen.

I chose my moment to tell Mum. She returned from the shops and shouted to me that she'd got some milk if I wanted my breakfast. I waited until I heard her talking to

32

Auntie Rita and then ambled into the kitchen. Auntie Rita was sitting at the table, smoking and rattling on about the new manager at work she didn't like.

'Nobody likes him,' she was saying. 'Straight out of university and he thinks he knows all there is to know about management. Comes into the staff rest room and—'

'So, did you find what you were looking for?' I interrupted.

'Are you talking to me?' she asked sharply.

'I asked if you found what you were looking for in Mum's bureau.'

'No, I didn't,' she said, looking embarrassed. Then she tried to change the subject. 'Anyway, Margaret, as I was saying, if this new manager thinks—'

I wasn't letting her off the hook that easily. 'An envelope, wasn't it?' I said.

'What?'

'When Mum was out at the shop you were searching through all the papers in Mum's bureau.'

'I was not searching through your mum's papers!' snapped Auntie Rita, colouring up again. She looked over at Mum. 'I wanted an envelope. That's all.'

Mum didn't say anything but I knew that she knew what Auntie Rita was up to. I could tell by the expression on her face.

Later, when I was in my room waiting for Auntie Rita to go, I heard raised voices coming from the kitchen. I crept to the head of the stairs and heard her complaining about me. 'Look, Margaret, I know he's had a difficult time but you need to speak to him. He says what he wants, he does what he wants and he comes in when he wants and he's very cheeky with it. There's no talking to him. He hasn't a good word to say to me and then he starts making accusations that I was looking through your things.'

'Well, what were you looking for in the bureau?' I heard Mum ask.

'I told you, I was looking for a pen.'

'I thought you said it was an envelope?'

'Pen, envelope, does it matter? I must say, Margaret, that if you can't trust your own sister, who can you trust? What I'm saying, is that if you don't have a word with that son of yours and start exercising some discipline, he'll end up in real trouble, one of these juvenile delinquents. He will, he'll go off the rails. I've seen it happen. Of course, you and Jimmy have always been too soft with him. I've always thought that. You've let him have too much of his own way. You've spoilt him and now the chickens are coming home to roost.'

'Have you quite finished, Rita?' asked Mum.

'I'm only saying what has to be said.'

'And since when have you been the expert on child rearing then, Rita?' Mum asked. There was a sharpness in her tone that I had not heard for some time.

'Pardon?'

'When have you had all the answers about bringing up children? If you were so good at it, Barry would still be with you.'

Wow, I thought, Mum was really letting her have it.

'Well, what a thing to say!' exclaimed Auntie Rita. 'That

was very hurtful of you, Margaret, especially after all I have done since Jimmy died. I've tried my best to support you, coming round most every day after work to clean and cook and make sure you are all right. I must say that when my husband ran off with that brassy, blonde tart from the petrol station and left me to cope alone, I could have done with that sort of help.'

'That's not fair, Rita, and you know it,' said Mum. 'I did what I could, you know that, but you insisted on doing things yourself. You wanted to keep busy, you told me that. And don't forget that Jimmy did all the decorating for you, sorted out the garden, fixed the fence at the back and the shed door when you had that break-in. He was always at your house doing something or other.'

'Yes, well that was the trouble with Jimmy.'

'What do you mean?' asked Mum. 'He liked helping people.'

'You don't need to tell me that. He was always fixing somebody's guttering, running old people to the hospital, mowing neighbours' lawns when they were on holiday, mending people's cars, doing all that charity work. He was never at home. If he had been, your Tom might have been better behaved.'

'That's why I loved him, Rita,' said Mum, 'because he was the kindest, most caring and generous husband on God's earth. He was always helping people and helping others killed him in the end.'

'You make him sound like a saint,' said Auntie Rita.

'He was a saint to me and a hero. There was no one like my Jimmy.'

'Mmmm,' hummed Auntie Rita, 'well, as I said to you at the time, I can't for the life of me understand why it was him who had to go back into that burning house.'

'You still don't understand, Rita, do you?' Mum asked her. 'You still don't get it. Jimmy went in because nobody else would. He was like that, he had to try. There was a child inside.'

'But he'd already been in the house—'

'I really don't want to go over all this again, Rita, if you don't mind,' interrupted Mum.

'Some would say it was a foolhardy thing to do, rushing back into a burning building,' said Auntie Rita. 'I mean he had a wife and child. Risking his life like that.'

'What did you say?' asked Mum.

'I said risking his life.'

'You said foolhardy, that's what you said.'

'Yes, well some would say it was a foolhardy thing to do,' said Auntie Rita.

'Some, being you,' said Mum.

'I didn't say that, Margaret,' said Auntie Rita defensively. 'But, as I said, some might say it was reckless—'

'I'd like you to go, Rita,' said Mum sharply, 'and I would appreciate it if you didn't come round for a bit. I'm sure Tom and I will be able to manage without you.'

'Not come round!' cried Auntie Rita. 'What do you mean, not come round?'

'Just what I said. I need some peace and quiet, Rita,' said Mum. 'I can't be doing with all this.'

'All what?'

'The noise and the arguments and you trying to run my life for me. I'm very grateful for all your help but I'll be all right. Just leave it for a while, will you?'

'You'll not be able to manage on your own. You know you won't.'

'I will,' said Mum. 'I'll have to. You've told me often enough that I have to pull myself together and that life must go on.'

'Well, if that's what you want, Margaret,' said Auntie Rita coldly.

'It is,' said Mum.

I could have jumped for joy and punched the air with my fist like a footballer after scoring the winning goal but then I remembered Martin Roadhouse. I would have to face him on Monday.

Five

'Is that the last we'll see of Auntie Rita?' I asked Mum. We were sitting at the kitchen table the following morning having our breakfast.

'Were you listening in yesterday?' she asked.

'I couldn't help but hear,' I replied, crunching my cornflakes noisily. 'You were shouting at each other.'

'Don't talk with your mouth full,' Mum told me.

'I heard what she—' I began, but Mum interrupted.

'We weren't shouting,' she said. 'Anyway, let's change the subject of Auntie Rita.'

'I'm all for that!' I said, spitting out bits of cornflake.

'Now, what are you up to today?' asked Mum.

'I've got some homework to do,' I told her. 'We have to write a story called *A Holiday to Remember*.'

'That's easy enough,' said Mum. 'You could write about Whitby.'

'And the marble?'

'It was certainly memorable, I'll give you that,' laughed Mum.

'No,' I told her, 'I'm going to write about when we went to that leisure centre in Scarborough and that woman got stuck in the water chute.'

It was one of the funniest things I had ever seen. This huge woman in a gold bathing suit thought she would slide down the water chute. It was really high and curled round and round down to the water. Dad said it was not a good idea when he saw her climbing the ladder in front of him. Anyhow, she shot off down the slide at a tremendous speed like a big bullet out of a gun but after the bend she must have started slowing down and then she stopped. She had blocked the tunnel. Dad was right behind her, of course, and he didn't know she was stuck because she was round the bend and he couldn't see her. He launched himself and set off after her really fast. He bashed into her halfway down and they both shot out at the end of the chute, their bodies sort of knotted together. There were arms and legs all tangled up. When they hit the pool together there was this almighty explosion of water. The attendant blew his whistle and ordered them both out for messing about in the pool.

'Your dad was so embarrassed,' said Mum, smiling. 'All those people laughing and that poor woman. I really felt for her. Your dad seemed to attract trouble like a magnet.' She looked down at the floor and suddenly looked sad. I guess it was what she had just said.

'And do you remember at the end of the holiday,' I said, trying to keep cheerful, 'when he came in from the shops with that melon underneath his coat, tucked between his legs, pretending he was a chicken clucking and flapping his arms and the melon fell out and bounced across the floor.'

'And broke the glass in the patio doors,' sighed Mum, shaking her head.

'I don't think that holiday was one your dad wanted to remember,' said Mum.

It was good to talk about the happy times. Mum and me hadn't spoken much about Dad like that since he had died.

'Well, when you've written your story,' she said, 'why don't you take your bike and go over to see Sinclair? You could do with some exercise.'

'I've told you it's broken,' I said. 'The gears don't work.'

Dad used to fix my bike. He loved fiddling about in the garage, mending punctures, sorting out the brakes, cleaning and polishing and oiling. Everyone used to think it was his bike, the time and trouble he took. Now my bike stood in the garage unused, rusting and broken. I just couldn't be bothered to do anything about it and anyway I wouldn't know what to do.

'You can come down to the supermarket with me, if you want,' said Mum.

'It's not open today,' I said. 'It's a Sunday.'

'They have Sunday opening now,' said Mum. 'Do you want to come? I've got a big shop to do today and I thought I might ask the manager if there are any jobs going.'

'You mean to go out to work?'

'Well, it would give me something to do instead of moping around the house all day. You wouldn't mind, would you?'

'I don't know. I've not thought about it,' I said.

'If I did get a job there I wouldn't be here when you got back from school. You'd have to let yourself in. And I might have to leave before you in the morning.'

'I'm not a little kid, you know,' I told her.

'So you wouldn't mind?'

'No.'

'And you'd help around the house a bit more?'

'I suppose so.'

Mum then played her trump card. 'I mean I could ask your Auntie Rita to come round and help out.'

'Get the job!' I cried.

Mum laughed. It was the first time in ages I'd seen her laugh like that. 'You're a funny one, you,' she told me. 'Just like your dad.'

How I wish that were true, I thought to myself.

'Well, I must be off,' said Mum. 'Are you sure you don't want to come with me?'

'No, I'll see you later.'

'There's plenty to eat in the fridge. Now, you're sure you'll be all right?'

'I'll be fine,' I told her.

I spent the morning writing the story.

In the afternoon I decided to go down to the park. I used to go there with Dad some Sundays. We would feed the ducks at the duck pond and sometimes listen to the band which played there on sunny summer afternoons. Then we'd go on to the playing fields and kick a football about. Dad taught me how to dribble and run with and pass the ball. I had got pretty good at football and was picked for the school team. Dad came to watch me play every Saturday and would shout from the sidelines. Once the referee came over and told him off for making too much noise. Dad looked like a naughty schoolboy. I hadn't played any football since Dad died.

I wandered down the long gravel path bordered by neatly tended shrubs and flowers and found myself at the children's playground. There were small kids, some with their fathers, swinging and sliding and jumping and balancing. I sat on a swing and pushed myself backwards and forwards and thought of Dad. 'Firefighter hero tries to save child in house blaze!' said the headlines in the paper. 'Brave firefighter dies in tragic blaze.' Not many people would have risked their lives and gone back into a blazing building to try and save the life of a child, a child probably like the little girl who was playing on the seesaw in front of me at that very moment. Yes, everybody had said he was a hero. Well, nearly everybody. Then Auntie Rita's poisoned words came into my head, eating away at my thoughts. 'I can't for the life of me understand why it was him who had to go back into that burning house. There were lots of other people around. What were all the other firefighters doing? Some would say it was a foolhardy thing to do.' And I remembered what Martin Roadhouse had called my dad. 'Stupid' he had said.

I must have been there for a couple of hours because when it began to rain and I headed for home, the clock on the church tower struck four o'clock. I didn't go straight home. I sat on a hard metal chair in the bandstand and watched the rain pour down, soaking everything and forming puddles on the paths. Dad used to say that if I practised really hard on my trumpet I would be sitting up there one day with the band. Since Dad had died, I hadn't taken the trumpet out of its case and had stopped going to lessons. What was the point?

'Rain's nearly stopped now, son.' The park keeper's voice interrupted my thoughts. 'It's about time you were heading off home. Your mum will be wondering where you've got to. I shall be locking the park gates in ten minutes.' I got up to go.

'Hey, you're the lad who comes to hear the band on Sundays, aren't you?'

'Yes,' I replied.

'With your dad. Tell him to bring you down next Sunday. We've got the army band playing here. Irish Guards. They're very good.'

'My dad's dead,' I said and ran down the steps of the bandstand, my face wet with tears and rain, and headed for home.

'You look like a drowned rat,' said Mum when I walked in through the door later that afternoon. 'Why didn't you shelter somewhere? Go on upstairs and get yourself dry or you'll catch your death of cold.'

'I was at the park,' I told her.

'The park, in all this rain?'

'I went down to the bandstand,' I told her. 'I thought a band might be playing.'

'What in this weather? Speaking of bands, I wish you'd start playing your trumpet again.'

'You didn't say that when I was practising.'

'Well, it would be nice to hear you again. Your trumpet's

not been out of its case since—' Her voiced tailed off. 'Well, off you go and dry yourself out, and then I've got something to tell you.'

'What?'

'When you're dry.'

'Tell me now.'

'Well, I've got a job,' said Mum. She was looking very pleased with herself. 'On the checkout at the supermarket. The manager was really nice. His name's Mr Peacock and he asked me a few questions and gave me a bit of a test and said he was very impressed. What about that then? I start tomorrow for a trial period. Of course, I've got to send in a reference and sort out the hours.'

'That's great!' I said.

'Are you pleased for me?'

''Course I am. You'll be able to get all sorts of free food.'

'Chance would be a fine thing,' she said, smiling. 'It will mean that you will have to look after yourself a bit more and help around the house.'

'I know, you've already said,' I told her, 'and you threatened me with Auntie Rita if I don't. It's called blackmail, you know.'

Mum gave me a big hug. 'What would I do without you?' she said. 'Your dad was so proud of you. When you were born and he held you in those big hands of his, this little pink scrap squealing and wriggling—'

'I sound like a piglet,' I told her.

'And he said it was the best day of his life. And you know, Tom, you're so like your father, a chip off the old block.'

No, I'm not just like my dad, I thought to myself. He was a hero. He never seemed to fear anything and he would have faced up to Martin Roadhouse, not stand around watching him pick on people and say cruel things. I knew he would have. He was that sort of person.

'Yes,' said Mum,' you're just like your dad.'

If only she knew.

Six

The following Monday morning I set off for school early. I didn't want to meet up with Martin Roadhouse on the way and have to listen to his taunts and feel his fat fingers prodding my chest. Sinclair came into the classroom just before the bell sounded for start of school with his coat and trousers all dusty and a red mark all the way around his neck. He had been crying and there were dirty smears all the way down his cheeks, where he had wiped the tears away.

'What happened?' I asked.

'It was Martin Roadhouse,' he said, trying to hold back the tears. 'He was waiting for me at the end of Richard Road and took all my dinner money. He emptied all my things out of my bag. Then he kicked me and punched me and pushed me over.'

'You'll have to tell Miss Fairclough,' I said.

'I daren't,' said Sinclair sadly. He looked really frightened. 'He said he'd hurt me even more if I said anything.'

'What are you going to do about your dinner?'

'That's the least of my worries. I'll tell Miss Fairclough I forgot my dinner money and bring it in tomorrow.'

'What will you say to your mum?' I asked.

'Nothing. I'll get it out of my moneybox. She'll never know. I'll come really early tomorrow so he can't get me on the way to school.' He straightened the collar on his shirt buttoning it up to cover the red mark and then began dusting down his trousers. 'I'll say I fell over in the playground.'

'Are you OK?'

He rubbed his stomach. 'He punched me really hard but I'm all right. I just don't want to talk about it.'

'Something's got to be done about him,' I said. 'Somebody's got to stop him.'

'Nobody dare,' said Sinclair. 'He's too big and tough.' He began massaging his throat. 'He's really hurt my neck as well.'

'You have to do something,' I said.

'You didn't,' he retorted, 'when he said your father was stupid and dumb.'

'That was different,' I said. 'He didn't hit me or steal my things. Anyway, you told me to ignore him.'

'And that's what *I'm* going to do,' Sinclair said, 'ignore him. I'm going to keep out of his way.'

I wanted to tell Sinclair that that was the coward's way out but then I thought of what I did when Martin Roadhouse went on about my dad. I wasn't much of hero then. I was as much a coward as Sinclair, just walking off. I had been frightened too.

That morning Miss Fairclough was in her usual cheerful mood until Martin Roadhouse started.

'Today we are going to look at riddles,' she said. 'Does any one know what a riddle is?

'It's when you go to the lav!' shouted out Martin Roadhouse. 'You go to have a Jimmy Riddle.'

'Don't be silly, Martin!' snapped Miss Fairclough. She wrote the word on the blackboard. 'Now, has anyone heard of this word before?'

We all knew what a riddle was but nobody put up a hand. We had stopped doing that the week Martin Roadhouse arrived and started making fun of anything we said.

'Gracious me,' said Miss Fairclough, 'you are slow for a Monday morning. Well, a riddle is a sort of poem with a puzzle.'

'Oh God,' muttered Martin Roadhouse.

'Did you say something, Martin?' asked Miss Fairclough.

'I said, "oh good," miss. I love poems.'

The teacher stared right at him for a time before she continued. 'Some riddles are of one line, others much longer, some easy to solve and others very difficult. On your desks is a copy of a poem I'm going to read out. It's a riddle, and I want you to see if you can guess what the poet is talking about.' Then she read:

> 'I have a hood and have a bonnet,
> But have no head to put them on it.
> I have a horn but cannot butt,
> I have a boot but not a foot.
> I have a body but cannot walk,
> I'm full of gas but cannot talk.
> I have a wing but cannot fly,
> What sort of creature do you think am I?'

It was easy. I knew it was about a car straightaway but said nothing. I didn't want to draw attention to myself with that fat smirking bully watching and listening. Like everyone else in the class I just wanted to keep my head down.

'Has anyone any idea what the poet is describing?' asked the teacher. No one said a word. Miss Fairclough sighed. I could tell she was finding this lesson really heavy going. Usually hands would be waving in the air with us all volunteering answers but not that morning. 'Well, I really don't know what is wrong with you all today. It's a car. Can you not see? Hood, bonnet, horn, boot, wing. They are all parts of a car. Let's see if you are any better at guessing what this next riddle is about. Don't let the title *A Close Companion* fool you into thinking it's about a friend. Follow it with me as I read it.'

Miss Fairclough read the second poem:

'As you sit all tense in the dentist's chair,
Eyes tightly closed, hands pressed together,
Listening to the whining drill –
I am there,
With you.

'As you lie in bed in the shadowy dark,
And outside a cold wind rustles the leaves,
And branches scrape the window like claws –
I am there,
With you.

49

'As you wade in the warm blue water,
Feeling the sandy sea bed soft beneath your feet,
And imagining what creature swims below –
I am there,
With you.

'I am the one who
Makes you tremble and sweat,
Makes your heart thump like a drum,
Makes your throat dry and your chest tight,
I am the one who fills your head with the most dreadful
    thoughts –
And you know my name.
Don't you?'

'What do you think the poem is about, Tom?' the teacher
asked me when she had finished the reading.

'I don't know, miss,' I answered quietly. I had a good idea
what it was but said nothing.

'Have a guess.'

'I don't know, miss,' I repeated.

'What about you, Simon? Any ideas?'

'I ddon't know, mmmiss,' stuttered Simon.

'I ddon't know, mmmiss,' mimicked Martin Roadhouse
under his breath.

'Martin, would you like to share what you have just said
with us all?' asked Miss Fairclough angrily.

'No,' he replied bluntly.

'Then I suggest you keep your mouth closed,' said the teacher, 'and keep your comments to yourself.'

'I didn't say nothing,' he told her peevishly.

'I'm not deaf, Martin,' said the teacher. 'So don't tell lies. Any more out of you and you'll find yourself outside Mrs Reece's room again.' He slumped back in his seat and began twiddling an elastic band between his fingers. Miss Fairclough decided to ignore him. At least he was quiet for once. Her eyes then settled on Sinclair.

'You look a bit worse for wear this morning, Sinclair,' she said, noticing how dishevelled he looked. 'You look as if you've been dragged through a hedge backwards.' Martin Roadhouse made a sort of snorting noise. The teacher gave him a look.

'I fell over in the playground, miss,' Sinclair told her, looking down.

Martin Roadhouse snorted again.

'Martin,' said Miss Fairclough, 'we can do without the animal noises.' She turned back to Sinclair. 'Straighten your tie, Sinclair,' said the teacher, 'and perhaps you can tell me what you think this poem is about?'

'Being scared,' he murmured. 'It's about being frightened of something.'

It must have taken Sinclair quite a bit of courage to say that, I thought.

'Yes, it's about fear,' said the teacher. 'We all have something that we are afraid of and—'

'I don't!' interrupted Martin Roadhouse suddenly.

'Really?' said Miss Fairclough. 'You're afraid of nothing then, Martin?'

'No,' he replied.

'Well, well, you are a remarkable boy. Unlike you, most of us have a secret fear. It might be spiders or bats or snakes or enclosed spaces, hospitals, heights, dentists—'

'None of them things frighten me,' he told her. 'But a lot of people are frightened of *me*.' Then he smirked and gave a low chuckle.

'And you think that's something to be proud of, do you, Martin?' asked Miss Fairclough.

'Yeah, I do,' he said.

She didn't say anything but just shook her head and sighed.

I stayed behind after school to help Miss Fairclough clear things away. I also wanted the opportunity of saying something about the bully; somebody had to, but it was Miss Fairclough who brought him up before I got the chance.

'Martin seems to be having a difficult time settling in,' she said casually as I helped her tidy the classroom.

'None of us like him, miss,' I told her. 'We all wish he had never come to this school.'

'Well, perhaps he has a lot to put up with at home, Tom,' she said, 'or maybe Martin is like he is because feels a bit left out of things. It must be hard starting a new school and trying to fit in and make new friends.'

'He hasn't tried to make friends,' I told her. 'And he doesn't fit in.'

'Have you tried to be friends with him?'

'No, and I don't want to either. I don't like him. He's always causing trouble, spoiling the lessons and being sent out. I used to like school before he started.'

'You had better tell me what he's been up to,' she said, perching on the end of her desk. 'Come over here a minute.' I did as I was told, keeping my head down.

'What's Martin been doing?' she asked.

And so I told her. It just spurted out. I told her about his picking on people, calling them names, hitting them. 'He's a bully, miss, and everyone's frightened of him.'

'There's nothing to be ashamed about Tom, being frightened,' said the teacher. 'We all feel afraid sometimes. We all have fears.'

'What are you frightened of, miss?' I asked.

She thought for moment. 'You promise you won't laugh,' she said.

'No.'

'Well, for a long time I was frightened of standing up and talking in front of people.'

'You were, miss? But you're a teacher. That's what you do all the time.'

'I know. Sounds odd, doesn't it? I always wanted to be a teacher but the thought of standing up and speaking in front of people terrified me. You might not believe this, Tom, but when I was a girl I was incredibly shy. I was bullied for a short time and know what it feels like. It was because of my ginger hair. "Ginger nut!" these boys used to call me and it made me feel different and scared. I hardly dared open my mouth. I would sit in the class knowing all the answers but too afraid to say anything in case I appeared a fool or was picked on. I did well in my exams but when I told my teacher that I wanted to train as a teacher she said I needed to be more confident, to speak out more, not be frightened to express an opinion.'

'So, what did you do?' I asked.

'Miss Wilkinson, she was my teacher, gave me a part in the school play. I told her I just couldn't do it – standing on a stage under the lights with all these eyes on me but she insisted. "There are occasions in life," she told me, "that you have to face your fear and overcome it." I only had a small part, just a few words, but I was terrified on the first night when it came to saying the lines in front of all those people. I sort of froze. And then something strange happened. I don't know where it came from but I suddenly heard myself speaking the lines. You know, Tom, we never know what we have in us until we are put to the test.'

'Yes, miss.'

Miss Fairclough smiled. 'I'll have a word with Mrs Reece about Martin. And don't worry, he won't know who told me. We'll get it all sorted out.'

The following day Martin Roadhouse's desk was empty when Miss Fairclough called the register.

'Has anyone seen Martin?' she asked, looking up and over the top of her glasses.

'No, miss,' we all chorused. There was a certain lightness in our voices.

Much to everybody's delight he didn't appear for the rest of the week. With his absence it was as if a huge weight had been lifted from off everyone's shoulders, a dark cloud swept away to reveal the sunshine. No Martin Roadhouse kicking people in the corridor, stealing their sweets, spoiling their games in the playground, coming out with his clever comments. All the class, including Miss Fairclough, seemed happier and more relaxed.

'No sign of Martin,' said Miss Fairclough after she had marked the register on Friday. 'I hope he's all right.'

Well, I hope he isn't, I said to myself. I know it was wrong of me to wish it, but I prayed that Martin Roadhouse had had some sort of terrible accident that would keep him away from school for good. Perhaps on the way back from school he had fallen in the canal and drowned or got some terrible disease or run in front of a bus and was now in hospital.

Just before the bell went for end of school Mrs Reece appeared and told us that Martin Roadhouse's mother had contacted the school to say he had glandular fever and that he would be away for quite some time. I felt like cheering.

'Perhaps the class could send him a get-well-soon card?' suggested the head teacher.

A sea of stony faces stared back at her.

Seven

I was feeling happier than I had done for a long time that day and was in a really good mood when I arrived home later that afternoon.

'Is that you, Tom?' Mum called from the kitchen when she heard me slam the front door.

'No, it's Burglar Bill,' I shouted back, hanging up my coat, 'come to steal all your money and your jewels.'

'What money and jewels?' Mum answered. 'And less of the sarcasm, young man.'

'Well, who did you think it was?' I asked, laughing.

'Come in the kitchen, Tom,' Mum shouted. 'There's someone I want you to meet.'

I found him sitting at the table with a mug of tea in his massive hands – a large man with grizzled black hair and a wide smile.

'This is Roy,' said Mum.

'Hi,' he said. 'How are you?'

'I'm all right,' I mumbled.

'Roy's a soldier,' said Mum, 'over here from America.'

'That's right,' he said. 'At the base at Ribbon Bank.'

'He helped me with my shopping,' said Mum.

'Least I could do,' said the man, giving her a great cheesy smile. 'You helped me with mine.' He turned his head to look at me. 'I shop at the supermarket where your mom works –

always Friday afternoons, regular as clockwork. I always seem to end up at your mum's checkout.' I didn't say anything so he continued. 'I dropped my groceries all over the counter and the floor. Coffee, milk, sugar, the lot – they went everywhere. Butterfingers, that's me. I caused quite a commotion.'

'I helped him pick them up,' said Mum.

'Later I saw your mom at the bus stop in all that rain and offered her a lift home.'

'I thought you said you should never accept lifts from strangers,' I said, ignoring him and looking at Mum.

'Roy's not really a stranger, love,' said Mum. 'He's been a regular at the supermarket for the last few weeks now.'

'We've got to know each other pretty well,' said the soldier and then added hastily, 'over the counter, that is.' I just stood there and stared. 'Your mom was telling me you're quite a soccer player, Tom.'

'It's called football in England,' I told him.

'That's right,' he said smiling.

'And I'm not that good,' I said.

'Yes, you are,' said Mum quickly. 'You used to play in the school team. They won the cup last year.'

'Is that right?' said the soldier.

'I don't play for the team any more,' I said.

'His dad and I were so proud,' said Mum. 'Tom scored the winning goal.'

'That's great,' said the man, all friendly like.

'It was a fluke,' I said, looking down at my trainers.

57

'We play American football in the States,' said the soldier. 'Of course we pick up the ball as well as kick it.'

'I do know what American football is,' I said. I could hear my own peevish voice.

'Sure you do,' said the man. 'I didn't mean—' His voice trailed off. 'I wasn't much of a player myself. I guess I was only in the team because of my size. Dropped the ball more times than I caught it. Roy, the "Man Mountain", they used to call me. You know—'

'Is there anything to eat?' I asked Mum.

'In a minute,' Mum said, glowering at me. There were two red spots on her cheeks so I knew she was angry but I was angry too. Who was this man sitting there where my dad used to sit? I didn't want him there. 'So when are you back home, Roy?' Mum asked the soldier in a really friendly voice.

'I don't exactly know,' he said. 'Could be in a few weeks, could be longer. This Middle East situation seems to be getting worse so, if they send more troops in, I guess I might end up in Baghdad rather than Houston.'

'Is that where you live?' asked Mum.

'Sure is. Texas born and bred. I'm just about getting used to the weather over here. Where I was brought up it was pretty hot and dry and—'

'So is there anything to eat?' I asked Mum, interrupting.

'Tom!'

'I'm hungry,' I said. Mum gave me such a look.

'Well, I guess I should be going,' said the soldier, rising to his feet. He was huge and broad and his hands were likes spades. 'Thanks for the tea.'

'Thank you, Roy,' said Mum. 'It was kind of you to run me home. I really appreciate it.'

'Anytime,' he said. He shook her hand. He looked at me as if wanting to shake mine but thought better of it. 'And I'll try to be a bit more careful next time and hang onto my groceries. See you at the checkout next Friday. 'Bye, Tom.'

Mum showed him out and I could hear her apologising for my rudeness and him telling her he quite understood and it was understandable under the circumstances. Then he was gone and Mum was back in the kitchen glaring at me.

'And what was all that about?' she demanded, her hands on her hips.

'What?'

'You know very well what, young man. Standing there scowling with a face like thunder and not a pleasant word to say.'

'I don't want him here,' I said.

'Oh, don't you?' snapped Mum. 'And since when do you decide who comes into this house and who doesn't?'

'I don't like him,' I said.

'And why is that?'

'Because I don't.' It was a pretty feeble reply but it was the only thing I could think of.

'Look, Tom,' said Mum, 'Roy gave me a lift home. Nothing else. He gave me a lift home because I was soaking wet and tired. He's not trying to run off with me or kidnap me. He's just a nice man who was friendly enough to stop and do a kind deed. Nothing more. That's what your father used to do. There are people in the world who are like that, you know, who see other people who need help and are happy to give it. He doesn't want anything. He's just being kind.'

'Well, I don't like him,' I said again.

'Don't be so stupid! You don't know him and you made no effort to know him,' exclaimed Mum. 'And the next time I invite someone into this house you be a bit more polite or you can go up to your room and sulk on your own. I really don't know what got into you, speaking like that. Your dad and I didn't bring you up to be ill-mannered and rude.'

'My dad's not here though, is he?' I replied. It was a spiteful thing to say and I felt sorry as soon as I said it.

'No, he's not,' said Mum angrily. 'And you don't need to tell me that. Your father's dead, Tom. He's gone. Nothing will bring him back. Nothing. We've just got to try and get on with our lives as best we can.' Her voice suddenly lost all its anger and she said so quietly I hardly heard. 'There's nothing else we can do.'

'I'm going to my room,' I said, nearly in tears.

'That's the best place for you,' she sighed.

In my room I took my trumpet out of its case and put it to my lips. I wanted to blow it really really loud, so loud the neighbours would bang on the wall, so loud the whole street would hear. I sat there pressing down the stops pretending to play it and then put it back in its case.

Later that evening Mum came up to my room. I knew she

would. She never liked arguments to drag on. Dad used to say, 'Never let the sun set on your anger.'

She tapped on the door.

'May I come in?' she asked.

I was sitting on the end of my bed. 'The door's open,' I said.

She came and sat next to me and put her arm around me. 'Are we speaking?' she asked. I nodded. 'We're a pair, aren't we?' she said.

'I'm sorry about what I said about Dad not being here,' I mumbled. 'I didn't mean it.'

'We all say things we don't mean, Tom,' she said gently. 'I'm sorry too for being a bit sharp with you. I suppose it was a bit of a shock you seeing someone in the kitchen where your dad used to sit. It's just that Roy was only trying to be helpful and he's one of the few shoppers with any manners. You sit at that checkout at the supermarket with all these people with full trolleys and they don't give you the time of day, they never smile and lots of times they never say thank you but just pile their shopping into plastic bags without even looking at you. Roy always has a smile for me and a few funny things to say. He's just a nice man.'

'You could always give up the job if you don't like it,' I said.

'It's not that bad,' said Mum. 'It gets me out of the house and takes my mind off things. I know it's been difficult for you,' said Mum, 'but time is a great healer.'

Things, I suppose, do get a bit better as time goes on, but the hurt and sadness never leave you. The wound never really heals. It's there all the time aching, until someone touches it and it flares up. You sometimes, for a moment, forget about the pain inside but then something triggers it off. Like the man at the bandstand mentioning Dad or the American soldier sitting at the table in the kitchen where Dad used to sit, drinking tea and smiling, just as he had done.

The following Friday I decided to go to football practice at lunch time. After Dad died I had given up on football despite Mrs Reece's nagging that the team needed me. Everyone was pleased to see me and I was picked to play for the team the following day. I got home from school in a good mood.

'Hi, Mum!' I shouted as I hung up my coat in the hall.

'Someone sounds happy,' came Mum's voice from the kitchen.

'It's Friday!' I shouted. 'No more school for two days.'

I scrambled up the stairs, changed out of my school clothes and five minutes later was in the kitchen with a big glass of milk and one of Mum's home-made biscuits.

'I've been picked to play for the football team tomorrow,' I told her. 'I have to be at school for eight o'clock to get the coach.'

'That's good,' said Mum. 'I was wondering when you were going to start playing again. What about the trumpet? Are you going to take that up again too?"

I changed the subject. The last time I played it was with Dad. 'You've had your hair done,' I said.

'Well, I thought it was about time.'

'It looks nice.'

'Thank you, kind sir.'

'Mum, do you think I could get my bike fixed sometime?' I asked. 'There's a shop in town which mends them.'

'Yes, of course you can,' she said, 'but how are you going to get in with it? I don't suppose they'll let you take it on the bus and it's too far for you to wheel it in. Look, I'll have a word with Jack at the supermarket. He comes on a bicycle to work. If I talk nicely to him, he might come round and fix it.'

'Great,' I said. 'Can you ask him on Monday?'

'I'll see what I can do,' said Mum. 'By the way, guess who came into the supermarket today?'

'Who? That American soldier?' I said glumly.

'His name is Roy,' said Mum, 'and it wasn't him I was talking about. It was that Mr Lee who owns the shop at the corner of Lillian Street. Do you remember, your dad told us about him? He was the man who had the accident in the toilet. I found it really hard to keep a straight face when he came up to my checkout.'

Dad had come home one night and told us this incredible story about a bathroom fire he was called out to. Mrs Lee had been decorating the bathroom and cleaned her paint brushes in a jar of turpentine substitute and then poured the contents down the toilet and didn't flush it. Mr Lee came in the bathroom soon afterwards, sat on the toilet and started smoking his pipe. He then tapped the remains of his pipe between his legs and down the bowl. There was a great flash when the turpentine ignited. As he lay screaming in agony on the floor, his wife sent for the fire brigade and Dad arrived just as the ambulance crew was taking the man down the stairs on a stretcher. When the ambulance men asked Mrs Lee how her husband had come to be been burnt in that particular part of his body, they laughed so much they dropped the stretcher down the stairs and the poor man broke a leg. What made it so funny was the way Dad described it. He was a great storyteller.

'I know it's nice to laugh, Tom,' said Mum, 'but when I saw what he was buying—'

'What?' I asked.

'Paint and paint brushes,' she told me. 'I know what your father would have said.'

'If his wife's doing the decorating,' I said laughing, 'I bet he's careful when he goes to the toilet this time.'

'I heard he'd given up the pipe after the accident,' Mum told me. 'It's not the best way of giving up smoking, is it?'

'Anyway, why have you had your hair done?' I asked. 'Are you going out somewhere?'

'I am, as a matter of fact,' said Mum. 'You'll be all right by yourself for a couple of hours or so, won't you?'

''Course I will,' I said. 'I'm not a baby. Where are you going?'

'Oh, just to the cinema.'

'Which one?'

'The Odeon.'

'What time will you be in?'

'Oh, about ten.'

'Who are you going with?'

64

'Tom,' said Mum. 'All these questions. You sound like my father when I was a teenager.'

'It's not Auntie Rita, is it?'

'No. It's not Auntie Rita.'

'Who is it then?'

'Well, if you must know, it's Roy.'

'That American soldier.' My heart sank. 'You're going out with that American soldier?'

'I'm not going out with anyone,' said Mum, colouring up. 'You make it sound like a date. He mentioned a film he wanted to see when he called in the supermarket this afternoon and asked if I would like to go with him.'

'I don't want you going out with him,' I told her.

'Now don't start, Tom,' said Mum.

'Well, I don't.'

'And since when do you decide what I can do and what I can't?' she asked.

'Well, I don't like—'

'Tom,' Mum interrupted, 'I am not arguing with you. I shall see who I want and that is that, and if you don't like it, well, it's hard luck. Roy is just a friend. I'm not going to elope with him to Texas. He's just a nice man and he's a bit lonely like I am—'

'But you've got me,' I said.

Mum sighed. 'I know I've got you, Tom, and I don't know what I would have done after your father died if I hadn't got you to help me through it. I'd have gone to pieces. I'm very lucky to have you. But life has to go on, love. We have to

65

make the best of it. Your dad would have wanted that. I know he would. He wouldn't have wanted us to mope about the house all the time, never seeing anyone or going anywhere. Since your dad died I've not seen anyone except the girls at the supermarket and I don't have a lot in common with them. All they talk about is boyfriends and clothes and television. There's more to life that that. There's your Auntie Rita, of course, but you know what happened with her. I'm just going out for an evening. Roy's not going to take your dad's place. Nobody could ever do that. He's off back to America in a few weeks and it's doubtful if we'll ever see him again. So can't you try and understand? He's collecting me at seven and you'll come down and speak to him, won't you? You will try and be a bit nice to him, for me, won't you?'

'I suppose so,' I said sullenly.

I wasn't nice to him when he called round. In fact I just mumbled a 'Hello' when I answered the door to find him there on the doorstep holding a large coloured box. 'Mum said to wait in the front room,' I told him and made to go to my room.

'Hey, Tom,' he shouted as I was halfway up the stairs. 'I've got something here for you.' I turned round. He held out the large coloured cardboard box. 'It's a kite,' he said, 'a box kite.' I didn't know what to say. 'You haven't got one, have you?'

'No,' I replied, not moving.

'When I was your age I had this kite, big yellow box kite it was. I used to spend hours flying it. Perhaps if I get over to England again I'll help you fly it.'

'When are you going back to America?' I asked.

'Pretty soon, I think,' he told me. 'Can't say exactly when. Then, after some training, I'll be off to the Middle East, I guess. Never been out there before. I'm a bit nervous to be honest.' He shrugged. 'Well, I'll leave the kite here in the hall.'

'Thanks,' I said and went up to my room and lay on the bed and stared at the ceiling.

A moment later Mum shouted up the stairs. ''Bye, Tom. I'll not be late. Lock the door after me.'

I heard the car doors slam and the motor start. Then they drove away. I felt suddenly so lonely and unhappy. And then just when I thought things couldn't get worse, Martin Roadhouse returned to school.

Eight

The bully sat smirking in his chair as Miss Fairclough called the register on Wednesday morning. She placed her pen carefully on the desk and looked over her glasses. She didn't look that pleased to see him back. 'Well, Martin,' she said, trying to sound cheerful, 'it's good to see you back at school and fully recovered. It can't have been very pleasant being in bed all week.'

'It was horrible,' he announced to everyone, still smirking. 'I was sick all over the place. Yuck!' He made a noise as if he were vomiting.

'Yes, well, now that you are back,' said the teacher, 'there's a lot of catching up to do. Perhaps you would like to borrow Thomas's book and copy out all the work you have missed and I think a few lunch times with me to go over things is in order.' That took the smile off his face and no mistake.

That morning we were doing art and Shruti Patel had just finished a really amazing picture. It was a scene in pale blues and greens showing a still sea with far-off purple mountains. Shruti was brilliant at art and some of her pictures had been framed and hung on the walls down the corridor and in the entrance hall. She had won a competition the previous term and had a certificate and a book token presented by Mrs Reece in assembly. When she started at our school, Shruti was shy but she used to sing as she painted. Her voice was clear and high and everyone liked to listen but she soon stopped when Martin Roadhouse made fun of her and said it was like listening to a cat being strangled with a piece of wire. He picked on her and said she ought to get back to the country where she came from. During the time he had been away, Shruti had started to sing again but that morning she had kept herself to herself and well out of Martin Roadhouse's way.

Anyway, when Martin Roadhouse saw Shruti's painting drying in the sunlight by the window, he accidentally-on-purpose tipped a whole jam jar of water over it.

'Oh, Shruti, I'm really sorry,' he said in a daft apologetic voice. 'I've gone and spoilt your lovely picture.' For the teacher's benefit, he said, 'I'm dead sorry. It must have taken you ages to paint and it was really good. Here, let me help you clear up the mess.' Then, with a fistful of paper towels, he obliterated the painting, which wasn't quite ruined.

'How did that happen?' asked Miss Fairclough sharply.

'It was an accident, miss,' wheedled Martin Roadhouse. 'I just sort of knocked the jam jar over as I passed. I'm ever so sorry.' Then he added with a slight smirk, which wasn't lost on Miss Fairclough, 'Accidents do happen, miss.'

'Yes, they do, Martin,' replied Miss Fairclough, 'and they always seem to happen when you are around. During your absence there have been no accidents.'

'I said I was sorry, miss,' blustered Martin Roadhouse. 'I couldn't help it.'

'I hope you couldn't,' said the teacher.

'I couldn't,' he said quickly. 'It was an accident, I told you that.'

'Don't you use that tone of voice with me!' snapped the teacher. 'We have had a very pleasant and peaceful time while you have been away. First day back and something happens. Now, get Thomas's book and sit down over there by my desk and copy out the work you have missed.'

'I haven't finished my picture,' he replied, glowering.

'Leave your picture,' ordered Miss Fairclough, 'and do as you are told or you will find yourself outside Mrs Reece's office for the rest of the morning. Go on, and start copying up. And take that look off your face.'

I had to smile. That's what Dad used to say when I pulled a grumpy face. My smile soon faded when Miss Fairclough told me to let Martin Roadhouse borrow my book to copy out the work he had missed.

Of course, getting on the wrong side of Miss Fairclough put Martin Roadhouse in a really bad mood for the rest of the day and he took it out on everybody who came his way. He trampled Debbie's coat on the floor in the cloakroom, snapped Sinclair's ruler and threw his pens all over the playground, pinched Simon Laister's sweets and twisted John's arm up his back until he gave him some money. At afternoon break it was my turn. He blocked the door of the boys' toilets.

'Where are you going, shrimp?' he asked, prodding me in the shoulder. I had thought of what I might do if he started on about my dad again. I thought I might hit him really hard in his fat smirking face but now it came to it, all I could do was stand there, frightened and ashamed. 'I said where do you think you're going, shrimp?'

'To the toilet,' I mumbled, looking at my feet.

'Oh no, you're not. I'm not going to let you, see.'

'Can I go to the toilet?'

'I said no!' He pushed me away from the door. 'You'll just have to cross your legs, won't you?' Then he roared with laughter. 'Or wet yourself. And if you don't like it, you can always bring your dad up to school. Oooo, I forgot you haven't got a dad any more, have you?'

'You leave my dad out of it,' I told him.

'And suppose I don't want to leave your dad out of it, squirt?'

I could feel my heart banging away in my chest and I was getting all hot. 'Just leave my dad out of it, that's all,' I said.

'Why, what are you going to do?'

I walked away. I felt such a coward. I should have stood up to him, lashed out at him, but I didn't. I was scared.

'Oi, insect,' he shouted after me, 'thanks for lending me your book to copy out my work. It's on your desk. I hope you like what I've written in it.' Then he roared with laughter again.

'You're pathetic,' I said under my breath.

He must have heard because he shouted at me down the corridor. 'You're dead! After school I'm going to wait for you, squirt, and teach you a lesson. You just wait. I'll show you who's pathetic. After school!'

I found my book on my desk screwed up with the pages ripped and bent back. There were doodles and scribbles all through it, silly smiling faces and rude drawings in the margins. He'd written 'CRAP' across my story *A Holiday to Remember*. I felt so angry and upset, not because he'd written all over my work which was bad enough, but because he had read about me and my dad and the happy times we had had. I could have shown it to Miss Fairclough – she would have known who had done it – but I didn't. I just put it in my bag and I'd tell her I'd lost it on the way to school. I would say nothing.

Anyway what was the point of telling her? She probably wouldn't do anything. I was mad with Miss Fairclough. 'We'll get it all sorted out,' she had told me and she had done nothing. Martin Roadhouse had returned to school just the same, in fact he was worse. 'I'll have a word with Mrs Reece about Martin,' she had said. Some good that had done. I wonder if she ever did have a word. One of Dad's expressions was: 'Words cost nothing.' He had been right. Instead of him sitting there all smug and full of himself Martin Roadhouse should have been outside Mrs Reece's room.

I know what my dad would have said if I had told him about Martin Roadhouse. He would have told me that you can't let bullies get away with it. If you do, they bully you more and more, they go on and on making your life miserable because you don't stand up to them. Bullies, he would have told me, have something seriously wrong with them because they find pleasure in hurting and tormenting others. They are just sad, pathetic people.

When I got back to the classroom after afternoon break Miss Fairclough took me aside.

'Are you all right, Thomas?' she asked. 'You look a bit down in the dumps.'

I wanted to ask her why she hadn't done anything about Martin Roadhouse but she probably knew what I was thinking because she said in a sort of whisper, 'I've not forgotten what we discussed about Martin. I've had a word with Mrs Reece and she has it in hand.'

After school I stayed in the classroom when everyone else had gone home. I could see Martin Roadhouse at the gates outside, no doubt waiting for me. After a while he got tired of standing about and started heading off. I waited until he had turned the corner and then set off myself but took a different route home through the park.

I was just turning down the path by the bandstand when I came face to face with him. He jumped out of the bushes and blocked the path and then he grabbed my coat roughly and yanked me towards him. He pulled me so close to him that I could feel his breath on my face.

'You didn't think you'd get away, did you?' he asked. I could smell his sour breath. He prodded me in the shoulder. 'I told you I'd get you. What was it you said? Pathetic? I'll show you how pathetic I am.' He turned me round and pushed me down the path ahead of him.

'Look,' I pleaded, turning to face him, 'why don't you leave people alone?'

He ignored me. 'I hope you can swim, because you're

going in the duck pond,' he told me laughing. 'And there's no fireman to pull you out.' I made to run off but he chased me and gripped my coat tightly and punched me in the back. I was frogmarched towards the water, my stomach churning and my eyes filling with tears.

The duck pond was dark brown with straggly, slimy weeds around the bank and a small muddy island in the middle where the ducks and water fowl nested. A large willow tree drooped its branches over the water.

But the bully had a surprise in store, for at the duck pond there was a man standing looking out over the water. He turned as we approached. It was Roy, not in his uniform, but looking so big and strong.

'Hello, Tom,' he said smiling, but keeping an eye on the boy who was with me.

'Hello,' I managed to say. There was a tremble in my voice.

Martin Roadhouse released me and eyed Roy suspiciously.

'This a pal of yours?' asked Roy, still with his eyes on the bully.

'Yeah, we're great mates, me and Tom,' Martin Roadhouse told him and putting his arm around my shoulder all friendly like. 'Who are you?'

'Just a friend of the family,' said Roy. He looked at me and I could see in his eyes that he knew that this big lumbering boy who was with me and who had gripped me so tightly by my collar was no pal of mine. 'I guess your mom will be wondering where you've got to, Tom,' he said calmly. 'You better come along. I'm going your way.'

Martin Roadhouse stayed rooted to the spot for a moment, looking at Roy who returned his gaze. 'I'll see you at school tomorrow, Tom,' he said with a sly smile on his face. He took his arm from around my shoulder and then, with his hands stuffed in his pockets, he set off down the path. He looked back before he turned the corner and waved.

I walked alongside Roy but didn't say anything.

'I often come down to the park,' he said after a while. 'It's really peaceful here and I can think. I'm a bit of loner, you see, Tom. I get on well with the guys at the camp but I'm pretty used to my own company and keep myself to myself.'

'I used to come to the park on Sundays sometimes with my dad,' I told him. 'We came to watch the band.'

'Yeah, your mom told me he was a real fine trumpeter.'

'Tenor horn,' I said. 'He played the tenor horn in a brass band.'

'Oh yes,' he said, 'it's you who play the trumpet, isn't it?'

'Not any more I don't,' I told him.

'You'll maybe take it up again one day,' he said.

We walked on for a while in silence.

'The young guy you were with,' he asked. 'He's not really a pal of yours, is he?'

'Not really,' I told him. 'He's in my class at school.' I changed the subject.

'Have you found out when you're going back to America?' I asked.

'No, not yet,' he said. 'All depends on some big general

when we go. We're all a bit jumpy at the base. We just want to get moving. All this waiting about makes us nervous.'

'And then you'll be flown out to Iraq?' I asked.

'That's the plan.'

'Where all the fighting is?'

'Yup.'

'Are you scared?'

He thought for a moment. 'I guess I'm a bit anxious,' he said quietly. 'Who wouldn't be?'

He was a big man, well over six feet tall with broad shoulders, long arms and a neck as thick as a bull's. It was hard to imagine that he would be frightened of anything.

'But you're still going, even though you're frightened?' I asked.

'Soldiers don't use the word "scared" or "frightened", Tom. Fearful, apprehensive, perhaps a bit nervous. It's the unknown which worries us most, what might happen, whether or not we'll be able to face what's in store for us, whether we'll let our buddies down.'

'Why are you going then?' I asked.

'Haven't got much of a choice, son,' he said. 'When you sign up for the army you have to go where you're sent.'

'Will *you* be fighting people?'

'I guess so.'

'Have you any medals?' I asked.

'Sure, I've got a chest full of decorations,' he said laughing.

'You must be very brave.'

'I'll let you into a little secret, Tom,' he said. 'Not one of those medals is for bravery. You see, you get medals for long service, for keeping your nose clean, good conduct and for being in a certain place at a certain time.'

'My dad got a medal for bravery,' I told him.

'Yeah, your mom told me,' said the soldier. 'He was some guy, your father.'

We walked on until we came to the gate of our house. 'I'm sure glad I was sent here to England,' he said. 'I'll be sorry to go. If I get over here again maybe we'll fly that kite.'

'OK,' I said.

He made to go but then stopped. 'And, Tom, if you want to talk to me about anything, well, I'm a mighty good listener.' Then he walked off down the street, leaving me at the gate thinking about what I should do.

Nine

The following day I kept well out of the bully's way. He picked on Simon in the morning and then Shruti in the afternoon but left me alone. Perhaps he wasn't going to do anything after all. Maybe the appearance of Roy at the park had frightened him off. I stayed in at morning and afternoon breaks in the school library to be on the safe side. Just before home time, however, the bully ambled over to my desk when Miss Fairclough had gone into the storeroom.

He had that nasty smile on his face. He prodded me hard in the chest. 'I'll be waiting for you after school,' he told me. 'And you won't have your bodyguard with you this time.'

When the bell rang for home time I waited in the cloakroom, looking down the school path, expecting to see him at the gates of the school. But Martin Roadhouse set off for home without waiting. I set off too, staying a good distance behind him and out of sight. I don't know why, but I decided to follow him. It might have been the way he kept glancing around to see if anybody was watching him that made me think something was not quite right. It didn't look as if he was after someone. It looked as if someone was after him. He turned down Ramsden Road and up the little alley by Lillian Street. He suddenly swung round but I managed to duck into someone's back yard out of sight. Then I peered through a crack in the fence. I knew that he was up to something.

At the dustbins at the end of the alley he stopped and glanced round again. I saw him dig into his pocket and drop something into one of the bins. Then he walked off. I waited a good five minutes before creeping down the alley and looking for what he had put in the dustbin. It was a purse and I had a pretty good idea whose purse it was because I had seen Miss Fairclough with one just like this. On the way home I went through the park and when I saw an empty bench with no one around, I sat down and looked inside the purse. It was Miss Fairclough's all right. There were her credit cards, a book of stamps and a photograph of two children but there was no money.

When I got home I went straight up to my room. I sat on my bed wondering what I should do. I suppose I could pop the purse into Miss Fairclough's drawer the next morning when she wasn't looking or say I had found it outside school or I could tell the truth – that I had seen Martin Roadhouse throw the purse in the dustbin.

'Tom.' It was Mum's voice coming up the stairs. 'Tea's ready.'

I must have been unusually quiet that tea time because after a while Mum asked me if anything was wrong.

'No,' I said. 'Why should there be?'

'Are you still mad at me?'

'About what?'

'Me going out to the cinema with Roy.'

'No. You can do what you want. You told me that.'

'It was nice of him to give you the kite, wasn't it?' she said.

'I suppose so,' I replied.

'Perhaps if he gets over to England again he'll come over and see us and take you to the park to fly it.'

'Maybe.'

'By the way, I had a word with Jack about your bike,' she told me, changing the subject.

'And is he going to fix it?'

'I don't think so. He's says he's too busy. Perhaps I could ask Roy to have a look at it. He's very good with his hands.'

'Except when he drops his shopping,' I said.

Mum smiled. 'Except when he drops his shopping,' she repeated. 'Shall I ask him?'

'You can if you want,' I said.

'He's a nice man, Tom. He's not going to be here for much longer. It looks like he'll end up in the Middle East after all.' When I didn't answer, she continued. 'It's a terrible thing is war. All that fighting and killing. I just hope he'll be all right.

'Will you miss him? I asked.

'Yes, I will miss him,' said Mum. 'As I said, he's a nice man.'

And a brave one too, I thought to myself.

The following day I got to school early, determined to put the purse back in Miss Fairclough's desk. She would have realised by now that she had lost it and when she discovered it at the back of the drawer, she would know straight away that someone had stolen all the money. But at least she would have back the credit cards and the photographs. When I arrived at the classroom Miss Fairclough and one of the cleaners were rummaging through the desks and looking in the cupboards. I knew they were looking for the purse. I peered through the glass in the classroom door and wondered what to do next when a voice behind me made me jump.

'What are you up to?' It was Mr Chapman, the caretaker.

'I was—' I started.

'You shouldn't be in the school this early. Off you go into the school yard until the cleaners have finished. Go on.'

I walked back down the corridor, watched by the caretaker. On my way out, I popped into the school library and pushed the purse between two books on a middle shelf. Someone would be sure to find it.

Before lessons started that morning the head teacher came into our classroom looking really stern. I knew what she had come for.

'Now, I want you all to listen very carefully,' said Mrs Reece, folding her arms tightly over her chest and staring at us. 'Put your pens and pencils down and look this way.' She scanned the class. 'I am waiting, Martin Roadhouse. When you are quite ready.'

'Sorry, miss,' he said in a smarmy voice. 'I was just looking though my homework.'

'I want to speak to you all about a very serious matter,' she said, ignoring him.

I looked over in the direction of the bully who stared back at the head teacher as if he hadn't a care on the world.

'Now, yesterday,' continued Mrs Reece, 'Miss Fairclough

couldn't find her purse. It's a small black and red leather purse. She remembers putting it back into her handbag after she had bought some petrol on the way to school. She remembers seeing it at lunch time yesterday. When she looked at home time, the purse had gone. We have searched the school from top to bottom this morning and there is no sign of it.' She paused and scanned the class. 'Has anyone seen it?' There was silence. 'Now that purse has not just vanished into thin air. What I think has happened is that somebody in this class took it out of Miss Fairclough's handbag yesterday.' Everybody was really quiet. 'Does anyone know anything about it? Has anyone seen another pupil near Miss Fairclough's handbag or acting suspiciously?' We all continued to stare in silence. 'Very well, I want everybody to empty his or her bag and put everything on the top of your desk in front of you.'

As everyone did as they were told, I thought to myself what a complete waste of time this was. I knew who had taken the purse and where it was and it wasn't in his bag.

Having poked amongst the contents on top, Mrs Reece pulled a really angry face. 'I don't want to have to call the police but make no mistake that if that purse does not turn up, I will. Has anyone got anything to say?' She again scanned the faces before her but no one said a word. 'All right, put everything away and sit up smartly. I intend to get to the bottom of this, you can be sure about that, and if someone did steal Miss Fairclough's purse he – or she – will be in very serious trouble, very serious trouble indeed.'

I watched Martin Roadhouse now, sitting there all pleased with himself with a silly smirk on his face. He suddenly turned his head in my direction and saw me looking at him. I looked away quickly but I knew he had seen me staring because, when I glanced back a few moments later, he was glowering at me and mouthing something.

At morning break I went into the library to see if the purse had been found but it was still there in exactly the same place where I had hidden it.

'I want a word with you.' It was Martin Roadhouse. He was standing right behind me. He must have crept up when I wasn't looking. He gripped my arm and squeezed the flesh between his fingers. 'You and me have got something to talk about.'

I tried to pull my arm away but his hand was like a vice.

'I don't know what you mean,' I said. My stomach was doing kangaroo jumps. Any moment I expected a punch in the stomach or a poke in the ribs or a kick.

'Oh, I think you do,' growled the bully. 'In class this morning. You were staring straight at me for ages.'

'I wasn't,' I said.

He stabbed me in the chest with his finger so hard it took my breath away. 'You were. You were looking at me when Old Reecey was rambling on about the purse.'

'I wasn't.'

He stabbed me again. 'Yes, you were. You were looking straight at me. Why?'

'No reason,' I said, bracing myself for another stab to the chest.

''Cos, if you know something, something about me and that purse then you'd better keep your trap shut because if you say anything, you're dead.'

'I don't know anything,' I lied.

'Well, if I find out...' He stopped short and quickly put his arm around my shoulder. He had seen Mrs Reece striding down the corridor towards us. When she arrived at the library she saw, for the entire world, two pals chatting away. He was really good at pretending, was Martin Roadhouse.

'I never knew you were interested in reading, Martin,' said the head teacher, raising a suspicious eyebrow.

'Pardon, miss?' he replied sweetly.

'I said that I didn't realise reading held such a fascination for you that you spend your breaks in the library.'

'Oh yes, miss,' he replied, giving her a great beaming smile. 'I love books. Can't get enough of 'em.'

'I'm very pleased to hear it,' said Mrs Reece. I could tell by the tone of her voice and the expression on her face that she didn't believe a word he was saying. 'Let's hope that this newly discovered love of books will lead to an improvement in your reading. Now you two should be outside on such a beautiful day. You can visit the library later. By the way, Martin, which book were you reading?'

'This one,' he replied, and without batting an eyelid, turned to the bookshelf and plucked the nearest book from the shelf. My heart missed a beat for he had picked a book next to the one the purse was resting on. Lucky for me neither the head teacher nor Martin Roadhouse noticed.

Mrs Reece took the book from his hands, read the title on the spine and smiled. 'How interesting,' she said. 'I would never have guessed, Martin, that you were so interested in flowers. Now, come along you two, into the playground and get some fresh air. There's plenty of time to choose books in your reading lesson.'

On the way down the corridor, when we were out of earshot of the head teacher, Martin Roadhouse whispered in my ear. 'We've got some unfinished business, you and me. I'll be waiting for you at home time.' Then he kicked the back of my heel and was gone.

After school I offered to help Miss Fairclough tidy the classroom. I decided that I had to tell her about the purse. I was the only one who knew where it was and who had taken it.

'You can have another look around for my purse if you like, Tom,' she said, 'but I've an idea it'll not turn up. Not in this classroom at any rate.' She gave me a look as if waiting for me to tell her something but I pretended to search for the purse, lifting desk lids and looking on the floor and plucking up courage to tell her. She came over and put a hand on my shoulder. 'You know, Tom,' she continued, 'if you or anybody else in my class know anything about what happened to my purse, they would tell me, wouldn't they?' I was certain that she was aware that I knew where her purse was.

'Yes, miss,' I said quietly. I took a deep breath. 'Miss—' I started.

Then I saw Martin Roadhouse glowering at me through the glass in the classroom door.

'Were you going to say something, Tom?' asked the teacher.

'No, miss,' I replied.

She caught sight of the bully, went to the door and opened it wide. 'Did you want to see me, Martin?' she asked.

'No, miss,' he replied, in that smarmy voice he was so good at putting on. 'I'm just waiting for Tom. We walk home together.'

She stared at him suspiciously. 'I see,' she said. 'Well, you get along. You don't want to be hanging around school on a Friday. Tom is helping me finish off here.'

'I don't mind waiting,' he said in a sharp tone of voice. He looked straight at me and his eyes were like slits.

'Martin,' she said firmly. 'Go home.'

He scowled but left.

'I think you were going to tell me something, Tom,' she said. I looked down. She waited for a really long time but when I didn't answer, she said, 'Well, you have the weekend to think about things. You had better get off home.'

I sat in the cloakroom for ten minutes, sitting on the hard wooden bench, feeling such a coward. When it had come down to it, I had bottled out, lost my nerve. I was just too frightened of what I knew the bully would do to me.

Ten

I just couldn't get to sleep that night. Every time I closed my eyes I thought about Martin Roadhouse and the purse. One part of me said to keep quiet, pretend I had never seen him throw the purse in the dustbin, put it right out of my mind, just don't get involved. But another part of me said that I had to tell Miss Fairclough, that I couldn't let the thief get away with it. Like it or not, I was involved.

I looked at my dad's photograph on the bedside table, lit up by the moonlight shining though the window. He seemed to be looking straight at me, accusingly. What would he have done? He would have done what he always said was the right thing to do – to tell the truth.

Once when I had been reaching for my football, climbing on the bottom shelf in the garage, I had brought down the top shelf. It had been stacked with paint tins and paraffin, cans of oil and bottles of weedkiller, boxes and tools, jars and canisters. The whole lot had cascaded down all over the wall and floor. I had not owned up to it and had told Dad I didn't know anything about it when he found the mess later that day. Dad had been really angry. 'Look, Tom,' he had said, 'accidents do happen. I'm mad that you pulled the shelf down because you should have had more sense than climbing up on a shelf which clearly would not hold your weight, but I am angrier and very disappointed because you decided to lie about it. I have always brought you up to tell the truth.' Tell the truth... tell the truth... tell the truth. I must have drifted off to sleep.

Next morning I overslept and awoke to see the time on the clock on my bedside table reading ten o'clock. I could hear someone tapping and hammering outside my bedroom window. I climbed out of bed, yawned widely, stretched and peered from behind the curtain. On the path outside was the American soldier. He was tinkering with my bike.

I dressed quickly in my old jeans and T-shirt, pulled on my trainers and ran down the stairs and out to the front of the house.

'Hello,' I said. 'What are you doing?'

'Oh hi, Tom,' he said in a friendly voice. He was squatting by the bike holding a hammer, his hands oily. 'I'm fixing your bike. Your mom asked me to have a look at it.'

'It's the gears,' I told him. 'They don't work.'

'I think I've found out why they're sticking,' he said. 'And your brake pads need adjusting. Could do with a bit of air in the tyres too.'

'My dad used to do all that,' I said. 'I suppose I'll have to learn how to do it myself now.'

'I guess you will,' agreed the soldier. 'Come over here and I'll show you what I've been doing.' I knelt down beside him and he explained how the gears worked and how to stop them sticking. 'You need to check your brakes and tyres as well, every time you go out. Don't want you crashing into anything.'

'I did once,' I said. 'Crash into something. It was a street-lamp.'

'Ow!' howled the soldier. 'That must have hurt.'

'I was showing off, riding down Ship Hill which is really steep and I took my hands off the handlebars. I lost control and ended up wrapped around this lamppost.'

The soldier looked up from tinkering with the bike. 'And were you hurt?'

'Broken arm and cracked ribs,' I told him. 'Dad said it was a pretty stupid thing to do.'

'He was right,' said the soldier, 'but then we all do stupid things at some time in our lives. I know I have. I remember once I was swinging on this rope which hung down from a long branch of a tree which grew near the creek. I guess I was showing off too. Anyhow, I was swinging backwards and forwards over the water and the branch snapped and I fell in.'

'Could you swim?' I asked.

'Oh, sure I could swim,' he told me, 'but I landed smack in the mud.'

I smiled. 'You must have looked very silly,' I said.

'Not really. I began to sink.'

'What happened?'

'Well, the more I tried to pull myself out, the deeper I sank. It was pretty scary.'

'Was there nobody around to help?' I asked.

'There were these three guys from my class at school on the opposite bank and I shouted for them to help me but they just laughed and laughed, fit to bust.'

'They didn't help you?'

'No, they didn't help me. They just laughed.'

'That was pretty mean of those boys,' I said.

'I guess it was. Anyways, I managed to grab hold of this tree stump and pull myself out, covered in mud and smelling like something the cat brought in. Got into real trouble when I got home. So you see we all do stupid things sometimes.'

I thought for a moment. 'Some people say my dad did a stupid thing,' I said, 'going into that burning house.'

'And what do you think?' asked the soldier. 'Do you think he was stupid?'

'No.'

'And neither do I,' he said. 'You know, Tom, there's always gonna be folk who comment and criticise and pass judgement and are keen to tell you what they think. It's a real mean thing to say that your father was stupid. Usually these people are sad, sour people, unhappy and jealous, people who have nothing better to do. My mom used to say that if you do a kindness, there's always gonna be folk who say you did it for what you can get out of it, that if you do well at something there's always gonna be folk who are envious of your success and if you're really happy with life there's always gonna be folk who resent that happiness because they lead miserable lives themselves. But my mom used to say be kind and happy and successful anyways. Don't let them get to you. What your father did, son, was brave, mighty brave. Not many people would have done what he did.'

'That's what my mum says,' I said.

'Well, she's right and don't you listen to them other folk.' He put his hand on my shoulder. 'You see, Tom, I know what you're going through, I know how you feel.'

'I don't think you do,' I told him.

'Yes, I do.' He sat on the ground next to me.

'No you don't,' I said. 'You didn't lose your dad when you were eleven?'

'Yes, I did,' he said quietly. 'My father was killed on my tenth birthday. He was thirty-one.'

That took the wind clean out of my sails. I felt awful now. 'Well, I didn't know,' I said.

'Of course you didn't,' he said. 'I never told you.' I was quiet for a moment, not knowing what to say.

'How did he die?' I asked quietly.

'He was killed in Vietnam. He was a hero, my father, like yours. You probably don't know much about that war. It was over thirty years ago and a lot of people back in the States want to forget about it. Nearly 50,000 American troops were killed in action. My father was one of them. He was a sergeant in the infantry. I'm named after him: Royston J Williams II. Pretty fancy sounding, ain't it? He'd only been out there a few days and his platoon was ambushed and he was killed. His buddy trod on a mine and he went back to help him. He got him out all right but took a bullet. My mom never got over it. She died a couple of years later in a car crash on the way home from the diner where she worked. They said she'd been drinking. You see, Tom, she wasn't as strong as your mom. She went to pieces when he was killed.'

'So what happened to you?' I asked.

'I was put in an orphanage for a while before different folks fostered me. I was an only child, like you, so I wasn't split up from brothers or sisters. I guess that would have been hard to bear. Anyhow, they seemed nice enough at first, these foster folks and treated me OK but I knew I could never be the substitute for the kids they couldn't have and they could never take the place of my mom and dad. I guess they were pretty disappointed with me. I wasn't clever or musical or good at sports and I didn't say much. I suppose I was a bit of a loner. Still am, if truth be told. After a few weeks in one foster home I was back in the orphanage, then I'd be shipped out to another.'

'Didn't you have any relations who could look after you?' I asked.

'There was my mom's sister, my Aunt May, but we didn't get on, so I didn't want to live with her.'

'My mum's sister's horrible,' I said, screwing up my face. 'Her name's Auntie Rita. I certainly wouldn't want to live with her. I'd sooner live with a vampire in a coffin.'

He laughed. 'Anyway, my Aunt May wouldn't have wanted me. She'd got kids of her own and didn't want another mouth to feed.'

'So what happened to you?' I asked.

'As I said, I was fostered with a few families,' said the soldier, 'and lost touch with my Aunt May and my cousins. I did write but I never got a reply so I haven't bothered any more. When I was old enough, I joined up as a GI and the army's been my family ever since.'

'Don't you have any family at all, then?' I asked.

'Nope, there's just me,' he replied.

'I'm sorry about your mum and dad,' I said.

'So you see, Tom,' he said, 'I do know what it's like to lose a father. I know about how angry you feel inside, angry at why it's your dad that had to get killed and not some other kid's. You keep asking yourself why didn't he just look after number one, take care of himself? Why did he risk his life like that? Why did he have to go back and help somebody else and get himself killed?'

'I sometimes feel like that,' I said.

'It's only when you're older,' said the soldier, 'that you begin to understand and you feel real proud, real proud of your father for what he did.'

'I am proud of what *my* father did,' I told him.

'So you should be, son,' he said. 'There are some people like that, like your own father, who couldn't have lived with themselves knowing that they might have saved someone's life, that they bottled out. So I do know about how lonely it sometimes gets and how empty you sometimes feel, how you miss him so much you get a pain in your chest. I know what it's like to see other kids with their dads and moms and know you'll never see them again. And it's no good people saying it'll get better with time, because it never really does. It never does.' He looked down and I could see tears in his eyes. 'Well,' he said, standing up, 'I'd better get washed up and be on my way.'

'Thanks for mending my bike, Roy,' I said, getting to my feet.

'No problem.'

'Can I ask you something?'

'Sure.'

'You know in the park when you said you were nervous about going to Iraq? '

'Yeah?'

'Were you telling the truth?'

'Sure I was. Who wouldn't be?'

'But you're still going, even though you're worried what might happen?'

'Haven't got much of a choice, Tom,' he said. 'When you sign up for the army you have to go where you're sent. I'm sure glad I was sent here to England, though. I'll be sorry to go.' He handed me the hammer. 'Your bike should be all right now. If I get over here again maybe we'll fly that kite.'

'OK,' I said.

He held out a hand as big as a spade's. I shook it. 'See you, son,' he said and headed for the house. As I wheeled the bike to the garage I felt it run smoothly along the ground. He had done a good job, I thought.

'Roy,' I shouted after him. 'Thanks.'

He gave a great toothy smile. 'My pleasure, Tom.'

Eleven

'Do either of you recognise this?' asked Mrs Reece.

I was standing in front of the head teacher's desk the following Monday morning with Martin Roadhouse by my side. On the desk in front of us was Miss Fairclough's purse.

'No, miss,' said Martin Roadhouse confidently. 'Never seen it before in my life.'

'What about you, Thomas?'

'It's Miss Fairclough's purse, miss.'

'Yes, it is indeed,' said Mrs Reece. 'It's Miss Fairclough's purse, minus the money that was in it. And do you know where it was found?'

'No, miss,' said Martin Roadhouse, shrugging.

I kept quiet and looked down at my trainers.

'Mr Chapman found it in the library hidden between some books when he was cleaning there last night.' She looked Martin Roadhouse straight in the face. 'He found it on the shelf near where you two boys had been sitting last Friday. Now that's something of a coincidence, isn't it?'

'Yes, miss,' he replied, barefaced.

'You will recall, that on Friday I found the two of you in the library and that I expressed some surprise that you were there instead of out in the sunshine.'

'I was reading, miss,' said Martin Roadhouse casually.

'Ah yes,' said Mrs Reece, 'reading a book about flowers.'

'I like flowers, miss.'

'And do you know on which shelf the purse was found, Martin?' she asked.

'No idea, miss,' replied the bully nonchalantly.

'The shelf where the books on flowers are kept. Now there's another coincidence.'

'Yes, miss,' he replied.

'Frankly, Martin, I don't believe you,' she said.

'I was, miss, I was reading,' he protested. His manner changed and he became defensive. 'I never took no purse. I've never seen it before and I've not touched it.'

'Didn't you?'

'No, miss.'

'I think you did,' said Mrs Reece.

'Well, I didn't,' he said, his eyes becoming slits. 'And you've got no proof I did.'

She drew in a slow breath. 'If I were you, Martin,' said the head teacher, 'I should be very careful what you say. I don't like the way you are speaking to me.'

'You called me a thief!' he said angrily. 'I shall tell my mam and she'll be up to school.'

'Well, I look forward to seeing your mother, Martin. There are a few well-chosen words I have for her should she come in to see me, about your attitude and behaviour since you started at Holgate School.'

Martin Roadhouse scowled.

'And what have you got to say, Thomas? You're very quiet,' continued the head teacher.

'Nothing, miss,' I said.

'Nothing?'

'No, miss.'

'Did you steal the purse, Thomas?'

'No, miss,' I said.

'Do you know who did?' I looked at the floor. 'Well, it's of no real consequence, the police will soon find out who the thief is. I really didn't want to have to call them but you boys have given me no alternative. I was hoping that the culprit would admit to taking the purse and we could deal with the matter within school.' I could feel my heart beating in my chest and my stomach churning. 'As soon as the police dust this purse for fingerprints we will soon know who the thief was, won't we? According to you, Martin, you have never seen the purse before and not touched it so there will be none of your fingerprints on it, will there? We will soon find out if you're telling the truth.' She picked up the telephone. 'All right, you boys, you may return to your classroom.'

'Er, miss,' said Martin Roadhouse, twisting uncomfortably on the spot.

'Did you wish to say something, Martin?' asked the head teacher.

'I want to tell the truth. I want to tell you what happened. It's been worrying me since the purse went missing.'

I couldn't believe my ears. He was going to admit to it. Martin Roadhouse was actually going to own up.

'Go on,' said the head teacher, still clutching the receiver in her hand.

'Well, it's like this, miss,' said the bully. 'I saw Tom take the purse.'

What! He was accusing me. Mrs Reece replaced the receiver with a clunk.

'I saw Tom take the purse from Miss Fairclough's handbag when she was helping Shruti clean up after she'd had an accident. She'd spilt some water on her painting. I tried to get Tom to put it back but he wouldn't. He took the money out and hid the purse in the library.'

Her eyes narrowed. 'And why didn't you tell me about this earlier or bring the purse to me.'

'Tom's my best friend, miss, and I didn't want to get him into trouble. I thought if I could get him to give the purse back it would blow over.'

'How very noble of you, Martin,' said Mrs Reece, 'to protect a friend.'

'When you saw us in the library, miss, I was trying to persuade Tom to give the purse back but he wouldn't.'

'And what have you got to say, Thomas?' asked the head teacher. I could feel two pairs of eyes boring into my head. 'Did *you* take the purse?'

'No, miss.'

'So, Martin's story is a pack of lies, is it?'

'He must have been mistaken, miss,' I said.

'Oh no, miss, I wasn't mistaken,' said Martin Roadhouse. 'I saw him take it all right. I told him to give it back. I did, miss. I mean, stealing's wrong, isn't it?'

'Well, here's an interesting situation,' said the head teacher.

'You say Thomas took the purse and he says he didn't. Someone's not telling the truth. I think overnight I will let you both sleep on it and we will have another little talk first thing in the morning. I'll see you both in my room then. And I promise you this, I will find out who did take the purse and when I do he will be in very hot water.'

On the way back to the classroom I tried to walk quickly ahead of Martin Roadhouse but he caught up with me, pushed me against a wall and gripped me by the throat. 'You say one word, one word, squirt, and you're dead. Best thing you can do is say you did it.'

Later that afternoon I went into town with Mum. When Martin Roadhouse saw her standing at the gate. He ambled past with that silly smirk on his fat face.

''Bye, Tom,' he called. I guess he wanted to warn me again about saying anything to Mrs Reece.

'Friend of yours?' asked Mum.

'No,' I replied.

I sat next to Mum on the bus wondering what I would say to the head teacher the following morning.

'You're quiet,' said Mum.

'I'm thinking,' I replied, staring out of the window.

'What about?'

'Things.'

'What things?'

'Just things.'

'It was good of Roy to mend your bike, wasn't it?'

'Yes.'

'He was out there over an hour fixing it.'

'I know.'

'Is it working all right now?'

'Yes.'

'What were you two talking about?'

'Things.'

'Oh, for goodness sake, Tom,' sighed Mum. 'What is wrong with you? It's like trying to get blood out of stone trying to get a word out of you.'

'I don't feel like talking,' I said.

'Well, I hope you'll be in a better frame of mind later on. I've asked Roy to come around for his tea. Is that all right?'

'Yes, it's fine.'

'I mean, it's the least we can do after he spent all that time sorting your bike out.'

'I said fine.'

'It's like talking to a brick wall,' said Mum to herself.

We were coming out of the butcher's when we ran into Auntie Rita. She was all dressed up in a coat as red as a pillar box and was carrying a shiny black handbag.

'Oh hello, Margaret,' she said, ignoring me.

'Hello, Rita,' replied Mum.

'How have you been?'

'Not too bad,' said Mum.

'I've been thinking about you.'

'Have you?'

'Well, of course I have. I mean you're my only sister and

I've been worried, you having to cope on your own.'

'I've got Tom,' said Mum.

Auntie Rita shot me a cold glance but still ignored me. 'I was going to call round, Margaret, but I wasn't sure of my reception. I mean after the last time when things were said—'

'It's water under the bridge now, Rita,' said Mum. 'I guess we both said things we wished we hadn't. Call round any time.'

I could have kicked Mum. I didn't want Auntie Rita calling round, getting her feet under the table again, filling the house with smelly cigarette smoke and making my life a misery. Things were bad enough at the moment. Having her there when I got home from school would be the last straw.

'I must say you're looking well, Margaret,' said Auntie Rita, relaxing a little. 'You're beginning to look like your old self.'

'As you pointed out, Rita, life does go on.'

'And you're working, I hear.'

'That's right, keeping myself occupied. How's that new manager of yours?'

'He left,' she said smugly. 'We made life a bit difficult for him so he asked for a transfer. Wasn't up to the job, of course, straight out of college and he thought he knew everything. We soon put him right, me and the rest of the girls.'

'Well, we must be making tracks, Rita,' Mum told her. 'We have a lot of shopping to do and—'

'Actually, I was going to pop round concerning something,' said Auntie Rita.

'Oh yes?' said Mum. 'What about?'

'This is neither the time nor the place,' said Auntie Rita, lowering her voice as if we were being overheard. She glanced in my direction. 'It's of a personal nature. Little ears and all that.'

'If there's anything to say, Rita,' said Mum, 'please say it. I tell Tom most things. He's the man of the house now.'

'Well, if you insist,' said Auntie Rita. 'Now don't go flying off the handle at me, Margaret, when I tell you. I've only got your interests at heart.'

'Tell me what?' asked Mum. I could tell by her tone of voice she was getting angry.

'And if your own family can't tell you, then nobody will.'

'What is it, Rita?'

'There's been talk.'

'Talk?'

'In the factory where I work.'

'About what?'

'About you, actually,' said Auntie Rita.

'And what could possibly interest all those gossipy men and women in your factory about me?' asked Mum. 'Am I that interesting?'

'It's because you are my sister that it was mentioned to me and I have to say I was quite taken aback.'

'And what was mentioned?' asked Mum. She was now looking angry.

'That...' She stopped as if thinking for the right words. 'It's that man you have been keeping company with.'

'Keeping company with?'

102

'I wish you wouldn't keep repeating what I say, Margaret. It's that American soldier. Maureen, who works next to me, says she saw you at the cinema with this soldier. And then Sid on packaging made some clever comment in the canteen. I wanted the floor to open up and swallow me.'

Pity it didn't, I thought to myself.

'And what business is it of Maureen's or Sid's in packaging what I do in my own time?' asked Mum.

'Well, I suppose Maureen thought I ought to know.'

'Why?'

'Because you're my sister and people are beginning to talk.'

Mum gave a hollow laugh. 'It's a pity Maureen and Sid in packaging haven't got anything better to do.'

'It's no laughing matter, Margaret,' said Auntie Rita, bristling. 'It doesn't seem all that right. I mean your Jimmy's not been dead for that long and you're seen out and about with this soldier.'

'I'm not marrying him, Rita,' said Mum. 'Not that that's any business of yours or your workmates.'

'I didn't say that you were. I'm just saying folk are talking.'

'Let them talk,' said Mum.

'And, of course, there's the other thing.'

'The other thing?'

'There you go again, repeating everything I say. I am not prejudiced, as you well know, each to their own I say, but he's coloured.'

'We are all coloured, Rita,' said Mum.

'All right then, black. He's a black man.'

'Thank you for telling me, Rita,' said Mum. 'I never realised that Roy was black.' Then her tone of voice changed. I had never seen Mum quite as mad. 'You know, Rita,' said Mum quietly, 'Jimmy used to say he found it hard to believe that we were sisters. He used to say how very different we were. He was right. In fact he was right about most things. You are a very cold and mean-minded person. It's such a pity there is so little in your life that you have to interfere in other people's and make their lives miserable. Don't call round, Rita. I don't really want to see you. You are a bitter, sour and unpleasant woman.'

Then we walked off leaving Auntie Rita open-mouthed and speechless for once in her life.

'She's an old cow,' I said as we headed for the bus stop.

'Thomas!' snapped Mum. 'Don't you dare use such language.' Then she said, 'Even if you are right.'

Twelve

The American soldier arrived later that afternoon with a small bunch of purple flowers. He was dressed in a smart blue jacket with silver buttons and grey trousers with creases down the front as sharp as knives.

'Why don't you two go into the front room,' said Mum, 'while I get the tea on.'

I sat on the settee opposite him. I noticed how big his hands and feet were.

'How's the bike?' he asked.

'It's working fine now,' I said.

'Remember to keep checking the tyre pressure and the brakes. We don't want you crashing into another streetlamp.'

'I will,' I said.

'And keep it well oiled.'

'Did you have a bike?' I asked.

'Sure did, not as fancy as yours, but I loved that ol' bike. You remember I told you about those three guys who laughed when I fell in the mud?'

'Yes.'

'Well, one day they took my ol' bike and threw it in the creek.'

'Why?' I asked.

'Because they were mean and they didn't like me. They were the school bullies and liked to pick on any kid who was a bit different. Well, they waited for me one day on my way home and took my bike and threw it in the creek. I watched it sink into the mud. I was pretty cut up about it. Anyhow, that was the last I saw of it.'

'You were bullied at school?' I was amazed.

'Yeah, I was bullied,' he said. 'I was kinda slow with my work and tall for my age and I was one of the few black kids in the school. Then there was the fancy name. There are four good reasons for the three of them to pick on me. Bullies pick on those who are different.'

'But you're big. You could have hit them and they'd have left you alone.'

'That's a myth that bullies are cowards and once you hit them back they leave you alone. It's just not true. And believe it or not, Tom, I don't like violence. Sounds strange coming from a soldier, doesn't it? If I can talk my way outa something I will. Force should only be used as a very last resort.'

'My dad used to say that,' I said. 'So what did you do?'

'Tried to ignore it but it went on and on, day after day. Some folk say that "sticks and stones may break your bones, but calling never hurt you." Now, I think that is a pretty stupid thing to say about bullying. You see, it's just not true. I tried ignoring all the name-calling and taunts but it gets to you. "Sticks and stones may break your bones, but calling can break your heart."'

I knew what he was saying was true.

'They said things about my dad and my mom,' he

106

continued. 'Cruel, hurtful things. Bullies like to see people suffer and enjoy tormenting other people with their name-calling and spitting and picking on them day after day, never letting up, making them feel pretty bad. One day, one of the boys started on about my father again. This time he was by himself. I'd had enough. I didn't hit him, I just grabbed him and held him, really tightly by the throat and told him not to say anything bad about my dad.'

'Did they leave you alone after that?' I asked.

'No, they didn't. This boy, his name was Cyrus Walsh, got his two sidekicks and they waited for me outside school and beat me up. I told my foster parents I had come off my bike but I wish I had told them the truth because they might have stopped it.'

'So they carried on bullying you?'

'Every day – nasty comments, spitting at me when I turned my back, calling me names, waiting to get me outside school.'

'So what did you do?'

'I put up with it for a while and nobody should have to put up with it. I know that now. Then I started skipping school, going off into the woods or down the creek. I let the bullies win you see.'

'What happened?'

'The principal called my foster parents and I was back at the orphanage.'

'That's just not fair,' I said.

'I just wish I had told somebody. Maybe they would have stopped it.'

Mum popped her head around the door. 'Tea's on the table,' she said.

I stood up making ready to go into the kitchen. 'Can you give us a minute, Margaret?' Roy asked Mum. 'I want to have a word with Tom.'

'And they say women gossip,' said Mum smiling. I could see that she was pleased that we were getting along.

When Mum had gone, Roy came over and sat next to me on the settee. 'Do you want to tell me about it?' he said.

'About what?' I looked down at my trainers.

'Come on, Tom, something's wrong. Anyone with an ounce of sense can see that. That guy in the park – he was no friend of yours, was he?'

'No.'

'Is he bullying you?'

I took a deep breath. 'Yes.'

'Thought so,' said Roy.

'I don't know what to do.' I could feel my eyes filling with tears. 'I don't know what to do.'

'I think you know what you've got to do,' said Roy. 'You've got to have the courage to tell someone who can do something about it, someone who can help you, to make it stop – your mom, your teacher, the head teacher.'

'I've told my teacher but she's done nothing and I don't want to tell Mum because it would only upset her. Anyway what could she do?'

'Knowing your mom – and I've only known her for a short time – I know she's the sort of person to sort things out.'

'If my dad were here—' I began.

'Tom,' said Roy, putting his hand on my shoulder. 'Your dad's not here but if he were I'm certain he would tell you that the bullying has got to stop. Sometimes you have to be brave enough to stand your ground, to speak out, to say enough is enough. You have to face what you fear. Being bullied is not something to be ashamed about.'

'It's hard,' I said.

'I know it's hard,' said Roy. 'Now will you promise me, Tom, you'll talk this over with your mom and get this sorted out?'

I nodded.

'Come on, you two,' came a voice from the kitchen. 'The tea's getting cold.'

'So,' said Mrs Reece, staring across her desk, 'now that you both have had time to think about it, am I going to hear the truth?' It was the following morning and Martin Roadhouse and me stood there side by side in front of her desk.

'Come on, Tom,' said Martin Roadhouse, looking at me and tapping his foot against mine. 'Tell Mrs Reece that you took the purse.'

I had thought about what Roy had said the day before, about not letting bullies get away with it, of having to stand up to them. And I thought about my dad. He would have told me to tell the truth. I suddenly felt angry. Why should I take the blame and be branded a thief? 'I didn't take the purse, miss,' I said suddenly. I could hear the tremble in my voice. 'Martin did. I saw him on the way home with it and I saw him put it in a bin. I brought it back to school and hid it in the library so it would be found.'

'That's a lie!' shouted Martin Roadhouse.

'Be quiet!' snapped the head teacher. 'Don't you dare raise your voice like that in my room.'

'He's a liar,' snarled the bully. 'I never took it. I never did.'

'Well, we will see, shall we,' said Mrs Reece, folding her hands on the desk in front of her. 'Here is an interesting development. Both of you say the other one took the purse.'

'He took it,' said Martin Roadhouse.

'Be quiet!' she snapped. 'And why did you bring the purse back to school, Thomas?' she asked me.

'Because it had Miss Fairclough's credit cards in,' I said, 'and some photographs and I thought she would want them back.'

'And what happened to the money?' asked the head teacher. 'There was twenty pounds in the purse.'

'Martin Roadhouse took it,' I said.

'Liar!' he exclaimed. 'I never took no money.'

'Well, I am inclined to believe Thomas,' said the head teacher.

'Why believe him, he's lying!' he spluttered. 'It's not fair, blaming me. Anyway you have no proof!'

'Don't raise your voice to me again, young man!' exclaimed Mrs Reece angrily. 'I will tell you why I believe Thomas. I did a little detective work on Saturday and asked in the shops around the school. And would you believe it, Mr Lee at the corner shop at the end of Lillian Street remembers a boy, a boy fitting your description, Martin, buying a large quantity of sweets. He remembers the boy in particular because he only had a ten-pound note.'

'It wasn't me,' said Martin Roadhouse, defiantly.

'Well, we will see about that. Would you like me to give Mr Lee a ring and ask him to call around and identify the boy in question?' She waited for an answer, drumming her fingers on the desk top, but Martin Roadhouse looked her straight in the eyes but said nothing. 'Well, would you?' she asked.

'Anyway, even if it was me, it was my money. I didn't nick it. My dad gave it me.'

'Oh, now it's from your father, is it? We shall be contacting your parents in due course and, no doubt, if you are telling the truth, they will be able to vouch for that fact. Or will they?'

Martin Roadhouse looked down at his feet. He realised it was no use denying it any more.

'OK,' he said, 'so I did spend the money from the purse but it was Tom who nicked it and gave it to me.'

'That's not true,' I said. I could hear the tremble in my voice. 'I never took the purse. He stole it.'

'Thomas, you may return to your classroom,' said Mrs Reece. 'And I have to say I am rather surprised at you. It would have saved us a whole lot of time and trouble if you had told the truth in the first place instead of keeping quiet.'

On the way back to the classroom I was still feeling angry and this time it was with Mrs Reece. Why did she have to make me stand in front of her with Martin Roadhouse next to me listening and tell her who had taken the purse when she

111

knew full well who the thief was? Now I was the target of the bully because of her. He would be out to get me.

Everyone in the class was eager to know what had happened but Miss Fairclough told us to get on with our work and stop chattering. I knew that Mrs Reece had been talking to her about the purse but she never said a word and carried on teaching as if it was any other day.

I was dreading Martin Roadhouse returning to the lesson but the minutes ticked by and there was no sign of him. Then, just before lunch time, we saw a large unshaven man with a bald head come marching up the path to the school. He looked like thunder. Miss Fairclough glanced out of the window and clearly recognised him.

'Thomas,' she said, 'will you collect Martin's things together and take them to the office? I have an idea he will not be returning to the classroom today.'

I was in the cloakroom looking for Martin Roadhouse's coat when he came down the corridor with the big man.

'You're just a waste of space, you!' I peered from behind the coats. They stopped and the man slapped him really hard across the face. 'You're a thief and a liar just like your good-for-nothing brother. And look where he's ended up.'

Martin Roadhouse started to blubber. 'I didn't mean to take it,' he spluttered.

'Oh, don't give me that. I've heard it all before.' He put on a wheedling voice. 'I didn't mean to. You never do mean to do things, do you? You're useless, that's what you are. Useless. As if I haven't got anything better to do than be called up to school by that sour-faced headmistress and told off like some bloody school child. Phoned up at work and told by the manager I had to get down to school, missing half a day's pay because of a great useless lump like you, who can't stay out of trouble. All that time your mother had to have off work when you was ill and now this. And I have to pay back the twenty quid what you took from some teacher's purse to spend on sweets. You fat greedy useless lump.' He smacked him again. 'I'm sick and tired of you and all the trouble you get into. School after school, you've been in trouble. You'll end up in prison like your brother the way you're going on. You thieving little git. Do you never learn? Do you?' I heard another slap.

'Don't hit me, Dad!' he cried. 'Don't hit me again.'

'I'll do more than hit you!' he shouted. 'Wait till I get you home. I'll give you a hiding you'll not forget in a long time.' The bully started to splutter something but his father cut him off. 'Don't start with your excuses. I've heard them all before. Now you're suspended and you'll be at home all day, stuffing yourself and lazing about.' He pushed him roughly. 'Go on, get out of my sight.'

I watched them head for the door. His father stormed on ahead, red and angry and breathing like an angry bull. Martin Roadhouse followed, whimpering. He didn't look the big blustering bully now, just a large pathetic figure. For the first time, I felt sorry for him.

113

Thirteen

Martin Roadhouse was away from school for three days. Mrs Reece never said a word in the Wednesday morning assembly apart from mentioning that Miss Fairclough's purse had been found. Our teacher didn't say anything either but I guess she realised that we all knew who the thief was.

Miss Fairclough took me aside at morning break on the first day of the bully's absence.

'I think you might have said what happened about my purse rather earlier, Tom,' she said. 'I'm disappointed with you. You could have saved a whole lot of time and trouble if you had told Mrs Reece the truth in the first place.'

It was easy for her to say that, I thought. She hadn't been threatened with being beaten up. I wanted to tell her that but I just said, 'Yes, miss.'

'And I think you will find,' she continued, in a confidential tone of voice, 'that Martin will be a changed boy when he returns on Friday and he won't be quite as' – she struggled for the right word – 'difficult. Mrs Reece has had a long talk with his father about the purse incident and the bullying and he says he wants to be informed if there is any more trouble and he will deal with it at home.' I knew exactly how his father would deal with it. I had seen him in action. 'I know Mrs Reece has had a word with Martin,' she continued, 'and she feels after he has cooled off for a few days and has had time to think about what he has done, he will have learnt his lesson and behave rather better from now on.'

Everyone awaited Martin Roadhouse's return with interest. I awaited it with dread. I knew that he would be out to get me now.

The bully came into the classroom on Friday, after his three-day suspension, didn't say a word to anyone and slumped into his chair. All morning he kept his head down, never spoke or put up his hand and Miss Fairclough left him alone. Perhaps he had learnt his lesson after all.

I was wrong. As he passed my desk at morning break he bent low and whispered in my ear. 'You are dead.' I could smell his sour breath.

'What was that?' asked Miss Fairclough.

'I was just saying hello to Thomas, miss,' he replied.

'Well, sit down,' said Miss Fairclough sternly, pointing to a chair right at the front of the room. 'You've missed enough work as it is. You can borrow Thomas's book and stay in over break to copy up the work we have been doing in your absence.' My heart sank. He scowled as reluctantly I handed him my book.

It poured down with rain later that morning. Water dribbled down the windows, gurgled in the gutters, formed great puddles in the playground and turned the fields into a muddy wasteland. This meant that I had a reprieve, for it would be a wet break and we would not be allowed outside and Martin Roadhouse wouldn't have the chance of getting me. It continued to rain all day so at afternoon break we had to stay indoors as well. Martin Roadhouse was unusually well behaved and said nothing but I felt his eyes on me and knew what would be in store for me after school. I watched the clock as it ticked towards home time and the inevitable meeting with the bully.

At three thirty the bell rang shrilly.

'Right,' said Miss Fairclough, 'put everything away, sit up smartly and then we can go. And do take care on the way home. No running across the road and be careful of the puddles.'

I thought about staying behind and offering to tidy the classroom, knowing what was awaiting me at the gates of the school, but I was mad with Miss Fairclough. She hadn't done anything really about the bullying apart from telling the head teacher who had 'had a word' with Martin Roadhouse and his father. It hadn't changed anything. My dad used to use an expression that 'fine words butter no parsnips'. Fat lot of good 'having a word' had done. I thought of hiding in the cloakroom, hoping that the bully would tire of waiting for me, but then decided that I had to face him at some time so set off for home.

Martin Roadhouse, as I had dreaded, was waiting for me, sitting on the low wall in the playground. He had a vicious look on his face. I made my way down the path looking straight ahead with a terrible hollowness in my chest and stomach. I could hear his footsteps behind me.

'Hang on!' he shouted. 'I want to see you!'

I ignored him and carried on walking quickly until I got to the school gates. There stood a figure, tall and broad. It was Roy.

'Hi, Tom,' he said. His eyes looked behind me and I guess were fixed on the bully who was just behind me.

'Hello, Roy,' I said. 'What are you doing here?'

'Just came to say goodbye,' he said. 'I'm back to the States next week and have to stay on the base until I go. I guess this is the last time you'll be seeing me, for quite a while anyway. I wanted to see you before I left. I've called into supermarket to say goodbye to your mom. I didn't want to leave before saying goodbye to you, too.'

I followed Roy's gaze as the bully sidled by. He stared at Martin Roadhouse like a cat watching a tank full of goldfish.

'So how are things?' he asked, as we set off walking.

'OK,' I said.

'Sure?'

'Yes.'

'You didn't mention anything to your mom, did you?'

'What about?'

'Come on, Tom, you know – the bullying.'

'Look, Roy,' I said, 'this is something I have to sort out for myself.'

'It's not the way, son,' he said, shaking his head. 'Unless you tell someone who can help you, the bullying will continue.'

'I promise if it gets any worse,' I told him, 'I will tell Mum, but not yet.'

'Why don't we go back into school and have a word with your principal?'

'No!' I cried. 'I don't want to do that. I know you're only trying to help me but you've got to let me sort this out for myself.'

'Look, Tom,' he said, 'I worry about you. You're a good kid. You don't deserve this.' When I didn't answer he shook his head. 'OK. OK. I'll butt out. I just hope things work out for you.' Then he changed the subject. 'Will you write to me when I'm in Iraq?'

'Yes,' I said. 'I'd like to.'

'And tell me what you're up to and how your mom's getting on?'

'Sure.'

'And don't you forget that we have a date to fly that kite of yours.'

'I won't. There's a good spot at the top of Winnery Hill where it gets really windy.'

'Winnery Hill it is then.' We stopped at the corner of the street. The soldier held out a large hand. 'Well, 'bye, Tom,' he said. 'I'll be seeing you.'

''Bye,' I said, shaking his hand. 'Be careful in Iraq.'

'I sure will,' he said smiling and walked away.

I shouted after him, 'Roy!' He turned. 'I'll miss you.'

The following day was a Saturday so now that my bike was fixed I decided to cycle over to see Sinclair. It had rained solidly the night before but that morning it was bright and

118

warm. The sun shone in an empty blue sky as I rode through the town and arrived at the park gates. I pushed my bike down the path bordered with well-tended flowerbeds and neatly trimmed lawns.

'Good lad!' shouted the park keeper from his little hut. 'I wish everyone would obey the "No Cycling" rule and get off their bikes when they come through the park.'

I waved. 'I'm coming down with my mum to hear the band tomorrow,' I shouted.

'Blues and Royals,' the keeper shouted back.

I soon arrived at the far gates of the park that led down to the canal. Down the bank stretched a narrow cinder path leading underneath a rusty red iron bridge and to the playing fields beyond. The path was usually dusty and riddled with potholes but that Saturday it was muddy and full of puddles after the heavy rain and impossible to ride along so I wheeled my bike.

The canal, dark green with a slimy scum on the surface, had an unpleasant, metallic smell. All along the bank, scattered amongst the army of tall stinging nettles and twisted briars, people had dumped rubbish. Black plastic bin liners spewed out rusting cans, sodden cardboard packets, shattered jam jars, plastic bottles, old clothes and discarded shoes. Someone had thrown a supermarket trolley into the shallow water at the side and it stuck up like the silver skeleton of some prehistoric creature. I stopped. I wouldn't like to fall in there, I thought to myself, imagining what might lurk beneath the slimy green surface. I sensed someone was

119

watching me and looking up saw a figure beneath the bridge. It was Martin Roadhouse standing in the centre of the path, his legs apart and his arms folded over his broad chest.

Well, this is it, I thought. I had been dreading this moment and now it had come. I gulped hard as if swallowing a piece of gristle and stood stock-still staring at him. I knew I couldn't make a run for it. I would have to wheel my bike back along the path, dodging the puddles and through the mud and he would soon catch up, so I stood my ground and waited.

Martin Roadhouse ambled towards me. He was in no hurry because he knew there was no escape for me.

'Well now,' he growled, as he came closer, 'what have we here?'

'What do you want?' I asked. I was surprised at the steadiness of my voice.

'You know what I want,' he said in a low threatening voice. He stabbed me hard in the shoulder. 'I've been wanting to see you. Unfinished business. Remember? You should have kept your trap shut.'

'Why don't you just leave people alone?' I said. 'You'll only end up in more trouble.'

The bully smirked. 'Wish your dad was here, do you?'

'Leave my father out of it,' I said, colouring up.

'Well, your dad *is* well out of it, isn't he?' he taunted. 'He's dead.'

I stood there, breathing heavily with anger and fear. I could feel my heart thudding in my chest.

'Nice bike,' said the bully, stroking the saddle. I was holding my bike in front of me, holding tightly onto the handlebars. 'Did your dead dad buy it for you? Pity it's going in the canal.'

'No, it's not!' I shouted, gripping it tightly.

'And then I'm going to give you a hiding you'll not forget in a long time.'

I looked straight at him. His little eyes, nesting in that fat puffy face, were as grey and cold as an autumn sky. I suddenly thought of what Miss Fairclough had said. 'There are occasions in life,' she had told me, 'that you have to face your fear and overcome it.' And I remembered what Roy had said: 'Sometimes, Tom, you have to stand your ground. You have to face what you fear.'

'Did you hear me?' asked the bully in that low threatening voice. 'I'm going to give you a hiding you'll not forget in a long time.'

'Like what your dad gave you?' I heard myself say.

'What?' he snapped.

'That's what your dad said he would do to you, isn't it?' I asked. 'Give you a good hiding?' My heart was thumping in my chest. 'I saw you and your dad when you came out of Mrs Reece's room. I was in the cloakroom, I saw it all. I'd been sent to collect your things and that's when I saw you.'

'You saw me and my dad?' he demanded. He was clearly startled. Then he gripped me by my shirt collar and twisted round the material so tightly I could hardly breathe.

'I saw you,' I said in a choking voice. 'I saw you when you

were sent home. I heard what your dad said to you and I saw what he did. I saw him hit you. Your dad's a bully just like you.' I wrenched myself free and backed away from him, holding onto my bike. 'You're just jealous of me because I had a dad who showed me how to do things and took me places and never called me fat and useless like your dad called you. I feel sorry for you. My dad was a hero and I was right, you are pathetic.'

Martin Roadhouse sprang at me. He was surprisingly quick for someone so big and heavy but I sidestepped. I don't know to this day how it happened but as he lunged forward I pushed my bike as hard as I could straight into him. The crossbar hit him straight in the stomach. It winded him and he fell back, losing his footing on the muddy path. The next thing that happened was like something in a film. He slithered and slipped and slid off the path, rolling down the banking and through the stinging nettles and into the canal, roaring like some wild animal. There was an explosion of green water. He disappeared beneath the surface and then emerged spouting and spluttering and gasping like some strange marine creature.

'Help!' he cried. 'Help me! I can't swim!' It was a desperate, high-pitched wail. He disappeared again, resurfacing only to take a spluttering breath before sinking a second time.

I watched fascinated from the path. The boy in the water was screaming and splashing about madly.

'Help!' he spluttered again. 'Help me! Please! I can't swim!' I thought of Roy, when he had told me about the time he had fallen into the mud and the boys had stood there and laughed. I wanted to do that now. To stand there and laugh, to watch the bully, who had made my life a misery, sink forever beneath the green slime. I would be rid of him forever. But then I thought of my dad and I knew what I had to do. I scrambled down the banking, scratching my hands on the sharp briars and yelled at him. 'Try and get to the bank!'

'I can't!' he screamed, still thrashing about in the slimy green.

I squelched through the mud and waded into the water. 'Grab my hand!' I shouted, stretching out. I knew it was the wrong thing to do to try and go any further and swim to him because he would only pull me under and we would both drown. I looked around for help but there was no one. Then I saw the sapling. It was a long thin strip of willow struggling to survive amidst the rubbish. I yanked it out of the mud. 'Grab this,' I told the bully. He reached out blubbering and spitting and grasped the lifeline.

A moment later Martin Roadhouse sat on the muddy path coughing and spluttering and rocking himself backwards and forwards. His face was as white as lard and his dripping hair a tangled mop. He really did look pathetic.

'I'd better go for help,' I said. My voice was surprisingly calm.

'I don't need any help!' he spat out. 'Just leave me alone! Leave me alone!'

'Are you all right?' I asked, putting my hand on his shoulder. He pulled my arm away and, panting like a carthorse, looked up at me and there was real hate in his grey eyes. I didn't really expect him to be grateful and that we would be great pals from then on but I knew he would now leave me alone. It wasn't so much the fact that I had saved his life and I could tell everyone about his terror of water that would stop his bullying; it was that he was aware that I knew all about his brute of a father and the shame and embarrassment he must feel.

Fourteen

After that, Martin Roadhouse did leave me alone. In fact he left everyone alone. I knew he hated me more than ever because sometimes I would see him staring at me in assembly or in the classroom with an expression that could kill. I never said anything to anyone about the incident at the canal or what I had witnessed from the cloakroom but, in a strange sort of way, I suppose he was afraid of me now, of what I might tell people.

Life got a lot better for me after that. I was made captain of the school football team and won a place with the County Junior side. I started playing the trumpet again and my school work got better.

'I'm glad to see that you are back to your old self, Thomas,' said Miss Fairclough one day as I helped her clear up after school. 'And I'm glad that Martin seems to have settled down and is behaving himself. No more bullying, I hope?'

'No, miss,' I said. 'No more bullying.'

'That's good,' she said smugly.

Of course Miss Fairclough thought that Martin Roadhouse's change was due to her and Mrs Reece 'having a word' with him and that he had stopped being so rude and nasty because of the trouble with the purse. Little did they know.

Life got better for Mum as well. She was taken off the checkout at the supermarket where she worked and made a supervisor. She looked like the cat with the cream when Auntie Rita called around one Sunday in one of her rare visits. I sat at the kitchen table pretending to finish a letter I had been writing to Roy but hearing every word.

'So how are things?' asked Auntie Rita.

'Very well, thank you, Rita,' said Mum.

'How's work? Not too much for you?'

'Oh no,' said Mum casually. 'Actually, I've just been made a supervisor.'

'You've been what?' exclaimed Auntie Rita as if Mum had come out with a rude word.

'I've been made a supervisor,' repeated Mum, looking very pleased with herself.

'But you've not been at the supermarket above a few months,' said Auntie Rita. I could see she was eaten up with jealousy.

'That's right,' Mum told her, 'but the manager, Mr Peacock, has been very impressed with my work.'

Auntie Rita said, 'For the past five years I've been at that wretched factory and had not so much as a pay rise. I can't tell you the times I've been passed over for promotion.'

'Really,' said Mum nonchalantly. 'And Mr Peacock has recommended me to head office for managerial training when the next course comes up.'

'Managerial!' exclaimed Auntie Rita.

'Don't sound so surprised, Rita. You said yourself I had to pull myself together. Well, that's exactly what I have done. I'm really getting my life back together and enjoying the challenge at work. And Tom's doing really well at school, aren't you, love?'

I looked up and smiled. 'I've nearly finished my letter to Roy,' I told her. 'Do you want to put anything in?'

'Just say I'm looking forward to seeing him again,' said Mum.

'I have to say, Margaret, that I'm surprised you're still in contact with that black soldier after all the talk. As I said—'

'Roy?' interrupted Mum. 'Oh, he's in Iraq at the moment but when he comes back over, which shouldn't be too long now, Tom and I intend to see a lot more of him.'

Auntie Rita pulled a sour face. 'Well, it's your life, Margaret,' said Auntie Rita, getting up to go.

'It is, isn't it?' said Mum, looking over at me and smiling.

I had received the first letter from Roy a couple of weeks after he had returned to America for training and I had written back and he became a sort of pen friend.

After the incident at the canal I had written him a long account and told him that the bullying had stopped and that I was much happier at school. He wrote a long letter back and said he was really proud of me.

I looked forward to the airmail envelopes dropping on the mat at weekends. I had seen in the news and read in the papers about all the trouble in the Middle East – the bombings and fighting and the American and British troops going out there. I took a real interest if there was anything on the television about the war. Roy's letter wasn't exciting or full of heroic exploits and he was not allowed to tell me exactly where he was and what he was doing but it was interesting all the same. Sometimes he would put in a photograph of himself in his uniform and once he sent a picture of a vast sandy desert and another time of a really huge spider called a Camel Spider that eats human flesh. I took it to school and the picture alone made Miss Fairclough shiver. I sent Roy some photographs of me on my bike, in my football strip and one of me playing the trumpet. Roy said this had been the first tour of duty when he had received letters and he looked forward to them as much as I did his.

'Roy will be coming back to England for some further training,' I told Mum one Saturday morning, reading from his latest letter.

'When?' she asked.

'When his tour of duty is over in a couple of months,' I said.

'It'll be nice to see him, won't it?' said Mum.

'Yes, it will. He said he'd take me to see Sheffield United,' I told her, 'and he wants me to explain the rules of soccer. He's going to help me fly my kite as well.'

Mum looked pleased. 'I'll cook a special meal.'

'You could ask Auntie Rita round,' I said mischievously.

Mum just smiled and shook her head.

One Saturday morning I arrived home wet and muddy but feeling pretty pleased with myself. I had scored the winning goal at the county football match and had been carried off the field on the shoulders of my cheering team-mates. I felt on the top of the world. As I turned the corner I saw an American army jeep parked outside our house. It must be Roy, I thought. Great.

I could hear voices coming from the kitchen when I opened the front door.

Mum must have heard me. 'Tom, will you come in here, please?' she shouted from the kitchen.

'I'm just coming,' I shouted back, hanging my coat up. It would be good to see Roy again, I thought. The thing about Roy was he understood – the only one who did apart from Mum – just how I felt about things.

I was not prepared for the scene that met me when I entered the kitchen. I expected to see Roy, at the table with his big smile. But it wasn't Roy. It was an American soldier – a sergeant, judging by the three stripes on his arms – in a light brown uniform with a chest full of medal ribbons. He was sitting in front of Mum at the kitchen table with his hands clasped in front of him, a pale-faced man with a puzzled expression on his face. Mum looked all weepy with red eyes and a runny nose and the soldier looked embarrassed.

'Tom—' began Mum

'What's wrong?' I asked.

'Sit down, love,' said Mum. She turned to the soldier. 'This is my son, Thomas,' she said.

'Hello, Thomas,' said the soldier, standing up.

'Sergeant Sobolewski is here about Roy,' Mum told me. Her eyes were filling with tears.

'Has there been an accident?' I asked. I knew something was very wrong by the expression on the soldier's face. 'Is he hurt?'

He coughed, a false nervous sort of cough. 'This is the part of the job I really do not like,' he told Mum.

'Will someone tell me what's happened?' I asked.

'There's no easy way of saying this, Thomas,' he said. 'I'm really sorry, son, to have to tell you that Sergeant Williams was killed in action in Iraq.'

'What?'

'One of his platoon was wounded,' said the soldier, 'and Sergeant Williams risked his own life to bring him to safety. It was a very heroic thing to do. Unfortunately, in doing it, he was wounded himself and later sadly he died from his wounds. I'm really really sorry.'

I slumped down in the chair next to Mum. She put her arm around me. I felt a terrible empty feeling in the pit of my stomach, the sort of feeling I had had when they brought me the news about Dad.

'Sergeant Williams was a quiet sort of man,' said the soldier. 'He didn't mix an awful lot and kept himself pretty much to himself. Didn't smoke, didn't drink. Regular sort of guy. But everyone who knew him said he was a mighty fine soldier, the sort of buddy that you would want beside you when things got tough. We have tried to get in touch with any family—'

'He didn't have any family,' I interrupted, rubbing my eyes.

'I didn't know that,' said the soldier.

'He was orphaned and spent most his life with foster parents or in an orphanage. His father was killed in Vietnam and his mother died in a car crash.'

'Well, Thomas, you sure seem to know a whole lot more about Sergeant Williams than we did,' said the soldier.

'I was his friend,' I said simply.

'We tried to contact his next of kin but with no success so what you have told me explains this.' He picked up a black briefcase and, placing it on the kitchen table, opened it. 'I found these letters in his locker. They were the only letters there. They're from you. I'm sure you would like them back.' He placed a bundle of letters before me.

'I wrote to him every week,' I said. Then I began to cry, great heaving sobs. I couldn't hold back the tears.

'He'll be all right,' said Mum, holding me to her and smoothing my hair. 'It's been a shock, but he'll be all right.'

'There's not a lot more I can say, ma'am,' said the soldier.

'No,' said Mum.

'Well, I had better be going,' he said.

'Thank you, Sergeant Sobolewski,' said Mum. 'It was good of you to let us know. Tom was really quite attached to Sergeant Williams. He was good man. We'll miss him.'

'He was that, ma'am,' agreed the soldier. 'One of the best.' Then he reached back into his case and held up a small shiny black box. 'I reckon Sergeant Williams would have wanted you to have this, Thomas,' he said. He held out the box.

'What is it?' I asked, sniffing and rubbing my eyes. I took it from his hands and slowly opened it. Inside was a medal, a

131

shiny gold heart-shaped medal with a broad purple and white ribbon.

'It's for conspicuous bravery,' said the soldier, 'awarded by the President of the United States of America for those who have been killed or wounded in action. It's the Purple Heart. That's a picture of George Washington on the front of it.'

When the soldier had gone I wanted to be by myself and went up to my room. I curled up on my bed and closed my eyes. I thought about Roy in the hot sandy desert and pictured him crawling through the sand, dodging bullets to help someone else.

It wasn't long before there was a light tap at the door. It was Mum.

'Are you all right?' she asked.

'Not really,' I said.

She came in and sat on the end of the bed. 'Oh, Tom,' she sighed.

'It's just that when things seem to be getting better,' I told her, 'something happens that spoils everything. I really liked Roy. He was my best friend.'

'I liked him too, love,' she said, 'but these things happen. I wish they didn't, but they do. I wish I had a magic wand that I could wave and everything would be all right but I don't. There's not always a happy ending.'

'But why did it happen to Dad and Roy?' I asked.

'I can't answer that, Tom,' she said quietly. 'You know, your father used to say that there are some people you meet in life that you are so grateful for having come across, good honest kind people who bring out the best in you and make you feel your own goodness. They are very special people, Tom, and we were very lucky to have Roy come into out life. I think he felt he was lucky, too, to have met us.'

I didn't sleep much that night. When the clock struck twelve on the clock in the distant church spire, the moonlight streamed though the gap in the curtains and lit up my bedside table. There was Dad as usual smiling from the photograph frame, his medal gleaning beneath. He was not alone. Next to him was a soldier with a great beaming smile and a small black box.

Thoughts whirled around in my head keeping me from sleep – thoughts about my dad and mum, Roy and Martin Roadhouse. I remembered Roy's words: 'I sometimes ask myself what I would do in the face of real danger. Would I run away or would I meet it? I wonder if I would do as your father did when he was faced with that big decision.' Well, he faced it and, like my dad, died trying to save another. Then there was my mum. She was heroic too, facing up to things, keeping going when her world fell apart, carrying on without Dad. I wasn't as brave as Dad or Roy, of course, but finally standing up to the bully made me feel good about myself and pulling him out of the canal made me feel proud about what I had done.

The next morning I went up early to Winnery Hill. It was a cold blustery Sunday and an icy wind rattled the bare branches of the trees and made my eyes water. The kite flew high in the empty leaden sky, soaring and sweeping, bobbing and dipping in the fierce wind. It seemed to have a life of its own. I felt the string cutting into my hand, the kite tugging as if struggling to be free. I released the string. The wind whipped the kite high into the empty grey sky and over the rooftops. Soon it was a small yellow dot in the distance.

About the Author

Gervase Phinn is a bestselling author and poet, teacher, freelance lecturer, educational consultant, school inspector, visiting professor of education and, last but by no means least, father of four. The majority of his time is spent in schools with teachers and children.